THE FOUNDATION

Published by Barrington Stoke
An imprint of HarperCollins*Publishers*
Westerhill Road, Bishopbriggs, Glasgow, G64 2QT

www.barringtonstoke.co.uk

HarperCollins*Publishers*
Macken House, 39/40 Mayor Street Upper,
Dublin 1, DO1 C9W8, Ireland

First published in 2025

Text © 2025 Melinda Salisbury
Cover design and illustration © 2025 Holly Ovenden

The moral right of Melinda Salisbury to be identified
as the author of this work has been asserted in accordance
with the Copyright, Designs and Patents Act, 1988

ISBN 978-1-80090-272-5

10 9 8 7 6 5 4 3 2 1

A catalogue record for this book is available from the British Library

Printed and bound in India by Replika Press Pvt. Ltd.

MIX
Paper | Supporting
responsible forestry
FSC™ C007454

This book contains FSC™ certified paper and other controlled
sources to ensure responsible forest management.

For more information visit: www.harpercollins.co.uk/green

THE
FOUNDATION

WILL ALWAYS WELCOME YOU

MELINDA SALISBURY

Barrington Stoke

CHAPTER 1

My mothers collected me from the police station. It was a bad sign that this was only the *second*-worst thing to have happened to me that day.

My mom took charge as soon as she arrived. She was a headteacher and used to dealing with unruly children. I just wasn't often one of them.

"Thank you, Officer," Mom said to the police officer who'd been waiting with me. "We're really sorry – Ivy isn't any trouble normally."

The police officer nodded and said, "She's very lucky, Mrs Finch. Today could have easily ended a different way."

Standing at my mom's side, my mum glared at me. "We'll be having a serious talk with our daughter, don't you worry," she said. "Nothing like this will *ever* happen again."

"We honestly thought Ivy knew better," my mom added. "We've discussed internet safety with her."

"Actually, I have something that could be helpful," the officer said.

She handed a leaflet to my mom while she explained, "A local organisation called the Ash Tree Foundation is hosting a camp for young people who have internet-addiction problems."

"I'm not addicted to the internet—" I began, but both of my mothers shot warning glances at me. I clamped my mouth shut, and the officer continued.

"As I'm sure you know, there has been a real increase in online crimes and incidents relating to AI lately," the officer said. "The Ash Tree Foundation is trying to educate young people about the dangers of online interactions and help them form solid relationships in real life. Or *IRL*, as the kids say."

I couldn't help but roll my eyes so hard that I saw the back of my own skull.

When my eyeballs returned to their normal position, I saw both of my mothers and the police officer staring at me. My mom looked *furious*.

"That sounds like *exactly* what we need," she said. Her tone of voice also said *wait until we get you home*. "And Ivy will definitely benefit from some real-life relationships, as she won't be gaming online again for a very long time."

"What?" I said. My mouth fell open. "That's not fair!"

"We'll discuss it at home," my mum said as she ushered me towards the door. "Thank you, Officer, for your help. We're all really grateful."

"My pleasure, Mrs Finch," the officer said, following us out. "Stay safe, Ivy. I mean it kindly when I say I hope I don't see you again."

We drove home in silence. The atmosphere in the car was heavy, like a storm cloud was hanging over us. It didn't break until we were back at the house.

I headed for the stairs, trying to escape to my bedroom.

"Not so fast," my mom said. "We need to talk, missy. This is serious."

She held the living-room door open. I sighed, walking past her and taking a seat on the sofa. My parents sat in their usual chairs – Mom on the right; Mum on the left.

"Do you understand what could have happened to you today?" Mom began. "Do you realise how bad it might have been? How close you were to becoming a statistic? I thought we'd taught you better than to meet up with random people you've only spoken to online, especially men."

"If I'd known he was twenty-two, I wouldn't have gone," I said. "He said he was fifteen, like me."

"Ivy, you can't just believe what people tell you on the internet," Mum said.

"I didn't *just believe him*," I protested. "I looked him up. I checked out his socials."

My mothers looked at each other, frowning.

"He was pretending, Ivy," Mum said. "His profiles were faked."

"We're getting off the point." Mom stood up and began to pace across the room. "Ivy, I don't think you understand how serious this is. He's a grown man. A twenty-two-year-old man knew you were a fifteen-year-old girl and *still* wanted to meet up with you. If the staff in the pub hadn't called the police, who knows what might have happened."

"Nothing would have happened," I said. "I pretended I needed the loo so we had to go into the pub instead of getting in his car. *And* I told the staff that I was underage. *And* that he'd lied about how old he was and that I was uncomfortable."

I sat back, folding my arms.

"That was very responsible of her," my mum said, turning to Mom.

"Thank you," I replied.

They both glared at me again, and I mimed zipping my mouth shut.

"It would have been more responsible if you'd called us," my mom said. "And we're getting away from the real issue here, which is that you lied to us, Ivy. You told us you were going into town to use the library."

"I didn't want to tell you I was meeting someone because I knew you'd be like this," I replied. "And if I'd known the staff in the pub were going to call the cops and not just kick him out, I wouldn't have told them either."

"Exactly," my mom said. "You don't understand the danger you were in."

"I do."

"No, you don't. Because if you did, you would have told us, or someone, that you were meeting a stranger. You would have let someone know where you were going to be. But you didn't. You lied about it."

"I'm sorry—"

"And that's why you're not allowed to play your games online any more," Mum continued. "You have to start living in the real world, Ivy. You can't keep escaping off to these fantasy lands. You need to engage with real people. You need to get a real life. You need friends."

Tears pricked my eyes and I blinked them away. "I have a life," I said. "I have friends."

"You have contacts on a screen," my mum said in a gentle voice. "They're not friends, Ivy."

"We're not saying you can't play at all," my mom added. "When you're ungrounded, you can still play normal games – the ones we buy you. But we're going to block the internet access for the console until you're at least sixteen."

My jaw dropped. I didn't care about being grounded. It's not like I went out anywhere anyway, as my parents had cruelly pointed out. But I *needed* to be able to get online when I was playing. At the very least, I needed internet access to download new patches and fixes for my games. I explained that to my mothers.

"We'll do that for you," my mum replied. "You can show us."

"But what about my teams? Mom, I'm in teams with people – they rely on me. I can't just disappear."

"Yes, you can," Mum said. "I know it doesn't feel like it right now, but everyone will survive. And you're going to this Ash Tree Foundation thing. There will be lots of kids there like you. Ivy, I know you can't see it right now, but you need this."

I slumped back against the cushions. My life was over.

CHAPTER 2

A week later, I was sitting at the back of an old ballroom in a big house called Chalmers Hall, surrounded by strangers. It was the first day of the Ash Tree Foundation Camp.

My mothers had managed to get me the last spot on it. They'd dropped me off an hour ago with my suitcase, told me that they loved me and they'd see me in four weeks.

I hadn't said anything, just folded my arms and refused to look at them until they left. I was furious with them for dumping me here with these people.

The receptionist at the Foundation had asked me to hand in my phone, and I'd put it in the box with a shrug, unlike one other girl who'd started crying, begging for just five more minutes. I didn't care about my phone. I cared about my games. Why couldn't my parents see that playing games was technically studying, as I was planning to be a game designer one day?

Everything in this ballroom was old and ugly: mismatched wobbly chairs, dark wood-panelled walls, the heavy moth-eaten curtains, the chandelier above us covered in cobwebs. There were gargoyles carved into the corners of the walls and ceiling, and a low cabinet displayed several ugly vases that were probably worth more than our house.

But the strangest thing in the room was Conrad O'Connell.

Firstly, he was the only boy here. But the really weird thing was that he was one of the biggest influencers in the country. Even I knew about Conrad O'Connell, and I only followed gamers. Yet here he was, onstage at a camp for teenagers with technology issues, grinning at us all – it must have cost the Ash Tree Foundation a fortune to get him.

Everyone was smiling back at him. Except for me.

I didn't buy into his whole act. How could he say "watch my online videos to learn why you shouldn't spend so much time online" and expect people to take him seriously?

"You think I'm a hypocrite, don't you?" Conrad said.

I looked sharply at the stage, panicked for a moment that he'd read my mind. The girl sitting on my left muttered, "Yep," under her breath.

But Conrad wasn't talking to me – he was addressing everyone. I waited a few seconds, then peeped at the girl next to me.

She had curly dark hair and was slumped in her seat. She must have felt me watching her, because she turned to me.

"Sorry, are you a Conrad fan?" she said, her voice a bit too loud.

The two girls in front of us twisted round and scowled in our direction.

"Shh." One of them held a finger to her lips.

When they turned away, I shook my head. "No," I murmured.

"Me neither," my neighbour said, lowering her voice a little. "My ex-best friend thought the sun shone out of his ... well, his everything. He always gave me the creeps. Ruby," she added.

It took me a moment to understand she was introducing herself.

"Ivy," I replied.

Before I could say anything else, the hall erupted into applause.

"Why don't we take a break and start getting to know each other?" Conrad said when it'd died down. He leaped casually from the stage.

Somewhere near the front, I heard someone actually sigh with happiness.

Conrad walked down the aisle between the chairs. Ruby curled her lip as he passed. Her sneer grew as a line of girls stood and followed him out of the hall like ducklings, leaving us behind.

Ruby turned to me.

"How does no one else see the double standard of Conrad posting videos every single day, sometimes *twice* a day, which all tell people they should spend less time online?"

I nodded. "It's clearly done for clout."

"Right?" Ruby said. "I tried to have this conversation with Deva – that's my ex-best friend – so many times. She was always like, 'But how else is he supposed to spread the message?' Ridiculous," Ruby scoffed.

"Completely," I agreed.

I wished my parents could see me. Here I was, talking to a human, maybe even making a friend.

"I don't get it at all," I continued. "You can't say 'we'd all be happier if we spent less time on our phones and computers' when your whole thing is getting people to like and subscribe to your online content. He's totally fake."

"I'm sorry you feel that way."

The voice came from behind us.

Ruby and I turned. Conrad O'Connell was standing in the doorway.

For a moment, no one spoke.

"I was just going to ask if you wanted to have coffee with us," Conrad said finally. "But I guess not. I'll leave you to it."

Then he walked away.

I leaned forward, burying my head in my hands, my face burning with embarrassment.

At my side, Ruby gave a low whistle.

"That's not ideal," she said.

I sat up. "Do you think I'm going to get kicked out?" I asked her.

"I think you should be more afraid he'll tell his fangirls you hate him and they'll hunt you down like a pack of dogs."

"Thanks," I said.

Ruby stood.

"I think I will get a coffee actually," she said. I assumed she was trying to get away from me, until she added, "You coming?"

"Are you sure you want to be seen with me?" I asked.

"I'm going to use you as a human shield if they attack," Ruby said. "That's why I need you to come."

I smiled. Ruby was funny.

We made our way into the next room, my stomach twisting with nerves.

Conrad stood in the corner, surrounded by a group of admirers. He looked over at us when we entered, and I turned away, pretending to be very interested in the refreshments.

The room had been set up like a buffet. There was a long station at the back with huge silver urns of coffee and hot water, stacks of mugs, plates of biscuits, and baskets containing crisps and fruit. There were tables to sit at, but no one was using them. The other girls on the programme were all crowding around Conrad.

But then I realised that wasn't true. In the far corner, a girl with faded blue hair sat by herself – the only person other than me and Ruby who wasn't trying to get Conrad's attention.

After Ruby and I had got our coffees and biscuits, I pointed her out.

"Looks like we're not the only ones in the I Hate Conrad O'Connell Club," I said.

Ruby grinned. "That makes three of us. Safety in numbers. Let's go and say hi."

The girl stared at us as we walked to her table. She looked older than us, and she seemed unimpressed at being interrupted.

But Ruby wasn't intimidated by her stare. "Hi, we're recruiting members for our I Hate Conrad O'Connell Club. Do you want to join?" she said, plonking herself down in one of the empty seats.

The girl looked at us.

"This is Ivy, our president," Ruby continued, nodding at me to sit down. "She just told Conrad *to his face* that she thought he was a fake. I'm Ruby," Ruby said. "And you are ...?"

"Freya. Freya Dixon."

Ruby's eyes narrowed. "Do you have a sister called Chloe?" she asked. "At Chalmers High?"

"Chloe's my cousin," Freya said.

"No offence, but I hate her," Ruby said.

Freya finally smiled. "I hate her too."

"If we're being honest, I need to tell you that one of my mums is the head teacher at Chalmers High," I said.

"Mrs Finch?" Ruby said. "She's all right. I used to be at Ashdown Lodge Academy. Chalmers is better."

"I went to Ashdown," Freya said.

"Small world. So, do you hate him? Conrad, I mean," Ruby asked Freya. "Or are you playing hard to get?"

I sipped my coffee as they chatted. I'd never been good at talking to people. I was fine online – my brain and my reactions were supersonic there. But in real-life conversations, most of the time I felt like I was stuck watching a tennis game, the ball flying back and forth so fast I couldn't keep track of who had it or work out where I could join in.

"Hello?" Ruby said. She was waving a hand in my face.

"Sorry, I spaced out," I said. "What did I miss?"

"Freya was just saying—" Then Ruby stopped speaking, and her eyes widened.

She nodded behind me, and I turned in time to see Conrad O'Connell arriving at my side.

"Can we talk?" he asked me. "In private?"

My mouth had gone dry. I nodded.

Conrad gave Freya a strange, almost angry look. Then he turned and headed to the door that led back into the ballroom. As I followed him, I heard whispering behind me. I looked round and saw the girl who'd cried when she'd given up her phone rushing over to Ruby.

Conrad waited until I was inside the ballroom, then he pulled the doors so they were just slightly ajar.

"I'm sorry—" I began to say, but Conrad interrupted me.

"You're right. I am a fake."

CHAPTER 3

"It wasn't supposed to be like this," Conrad said, and gave me an embarrassed smile. "Saving the planet is what I really care about. I started telling people to put their phones down and look at the world around them. But every time I did, I got more likes and comments and follows. Then I started getting sponsorship and collaboration deals. So now I'm the guy who's famous online for telling people to log off. Which means you're right. I'm a fake."

"I didn't mean for you to hear me," I said.

"Really I'm glad there's at least one person here who doesn't think I'm amazing," Conrad said, and gave a grim smile.

"Why are you here?" I asked. "Is this a sponsorship thing?"

Conrad shook his head. "The Ash Tree Foundation is run by my family," he said, his cheeks flushing pink.

"Wait. This is your house?" I said. "You live here?"

Conrad shook his head. "It's my aunt's house. She decided when she moved here that she wanted to do some real good in the community. She hosted a performing arts camp here last summer, for free, and she was going to do that again. But then a lot of technology stuff happened in the local area, and my aunt was worried about it. And as I'm pretty well known for being anti-tech, it all came together. My aunt decided to host a free camp for people who need help in breaking the hold their phones have over them. And here I am." He shrugged.

"What do we have to do while we're here?" I asked him. "No one has said what happens yet."

Conrad grinned. "Don't you want to wait for the proper induction this afternoon?"

"I don't like surprises," I replied.

Conrad looked to the doors, where the other girls were now visible through the gap, wanting him back.

He moved nearer to me so they couldn't hear him.

Being this close to him meant I could see the faint freckles over his nose, the black ring around his brown irises. His hair was styled carefully – messy, but not *too* messy, a little long, covering his ears. He *was* good-looking, I admitted to myself. I could see why people liked to watch his videos.

When Conrad spoke, his voice was soft.

"Basically, it's a technology detox. There are going to be activities, stuff outside in the grounds, art and music and cookery inside. The idea is you spend four weeks without your phones, speaking to other people and doing practical things with your hands and bodies."

As he said "and bodies", I felt another blush creep up my neck, reddening my cheeks. I hated myself.

"Everything OK?" This new voice startled me, and I looked at the door. A young-looking woman was staring at us. She had white-blonde hair pulled back into a severe knot at the base of her neck. Everything she wore was white too – a loose, floaty white skirt and a white shirt that tied at the front. Hanging from her neck, almost to her waist, was a silver chain with a large silver tree pendant on the end.

"It's fine, Dagmar," Conrad said. "This is Ivy."

"Hi, Ivy." The woman smiled at me. "I'd like to start the next session, if you're finished in here." She gave Conrad a meaningful look.

"Go ahead," Conrad replied.

The woman peered at us, frowned and then left.

"That's my aunt Dagmar," Conrad explained before I could ask. "She's the programme leader. I'd better let her start or she'll get moody. See you soon, Ivy."

He smiled and headed out of the ballroom, leaving me feeling like I was on fire.

A moment later, the ballroom doors were pushed wide open again. Everyone came back inside, all of them staring at me as they returned to their seats. Conrad and Dagmar entered after them, and Conrad shot me a quick smile.

"What did he want?" Ruby asked as she and Freya came to join me. "Are they sending you home?"

"No. He wanted to tell me I was right. That he thinks he's a fake too."

"Seriously?" Ruby asked. Her face was doubtful as we moved back to our chairs.

I sat next to her.

"He said he started out trying to be an eco-influencer," I explained. "But his platform didn't really take off until he talked about the anti-tech stuff."

"That's true," Freya said, sitting on Ruby's other side.

Ruby and I turned to her.

"It's what I used to do – eco-posting," Freya went on. "Not that anyone ever followed me until ..." She paused. "He really was an eco-influencer for a while. We started at the same time."

I wondered if that was why she was avoiding him, and why he'd looked at her so angrily. Maybe they'd been competing with each other.

A woman loudly cleared her throat, and I faced the front, where Conrad was standing on the stage with Dagmar.

"I hope you've all had a warm welcome," she said, stepping forward. "My name is Dagmar Nilsson, and I'm the programme leader here at the Ash Tree Foundation. We're so happy to have you all with us. I want you to know that the entire Foundation is deeply impressed by your bravery and your commitment to becoming your best selves."

Ruby gave a soft snort, and Freya elbowed her.

Dagmar frowned in our direction.

"I want to tell you a little about what you've got yourselves into," Dagmar went on. "I'm sure you'll all be relieved to know there are no formal events while you're here. You're not expected to attend lessons or lectures about how bad technology is."

Dagmar rolled her eyes, and we all laughed politely.

"That's not what we're about," Dagmar said. "But, while there's no obligation to join in, you'll get out of this what you put in." She shot Ruby a pointed look. "You're not here because you're being punished. You're here because society has stolen from you. Your time and your thoughts, your focus and your sense of self. We want to help you take that back. Here are the timetables ..."

She paused to nod at two people who'd silently entered the room and begun passing out sheets of paper. Like Dagmar, they wore white.

"I really hope to see you all joining in and making the most of this opportunity," Dagmar finished.

When Conrad began to clap, so did everyone else.

I took a timetable and looked at it. Around me, everyone was doing the same, and the room got louder as people found activities they liked and started to make plans.

"Conrad said he's running some of the sessions," a red-headed girl in front of us said to the girl next to her. "Do you think he'll do the birdwatching?"

"That's a 'no' to birdwatching then," Ruby muttered, and they gave her a dirty look. "I think archery – I might need the self-defence skills, and I can put it on my acting CV. Creative writing too – I have a script I've been meaning to start. And maybe cookery – my mum runs a catering business, and you'd think that would mean there'd be loads around to eat, but it's all buffet food. Sometimes I want a proper dinner."

"So you're signing up for stuff?" I said.

Ruby nodded. "I want to be my best self, Ivy," she said, in a scarily good impression of Dagmar Nilsson. "And it's all free. What else am I going to do while I'm here?"

On her other side, Freya was nodding. "I've picked sewing. I'd really like to be able to make my own clothes. I'm done with fast fashion. I'd like pottery too, but it's at the same time as swimming, and since they closed the town pool, I never get to swim any more. And I think I'll do cooking as well."

I looked again at the timetable.

"Cooking does sound fun," I said. "Both of my mums are really bad at it. Orienteering maybe. Whenever I play a game with a map, I find them really hard to read. Orienteering might help. What's forest bathing?"

"I think it's sitting under a tree, soaking up vibes," Ruby said. "Dagmar looks like a forest-bathing fan. She has that whole Earth Mother thing going on."

I glanced over at Dagmar and wrinkled my nose. She seemed OK, but I didn't think I wanted to sit under trees with her.

"How many activities can we do?" I asked.

Ruby and Freya shrugged, so I put my hand up.

Conrad noticed and nudged Dagmar.

"Ivy," she said. "Do you have a question?"

"How many activities can we pick?"

Dagmar beamed at me as if I'd really pleased her.

"A great question," Dagmar said. "We recommend a maximum of three, but once you've started a course, you can't swap to another, so think very carefully about what you're interested in. Once you're sure, there are sign-up sheets at the back of the room. A lot of the courses have limited group numbers for health-and-safety reasons, so—"

Before she could finish, girls started to rise and race to the back, pushing each other out of the way to sign up.

"They're all betting on Conrad running the nature ones," Freya said with a look of disgust.

I turned around to find Conrad watching me. He smiled, and I felt something in my stomach flutter.

*

We waited until the others had finished before we checked the sign-up sheets. Everyone else had gone to find their bedrooms and unpack.

Almost everything to do with nature was already full up, as Freya had predicted. Archery and yoga were full too. No one had signed up for forest bathing, and I couldn't find the list for orienteering at all.

"There goes my chance to be Robin Hood," Ruby said sadly as she added her name to the cooking list under Freya's. "Maybe I'll do sewing too. I could make my own costumes then."

I signed up for cookery, then stared at what was left. I wasn't interested in any of it.

"Are you going to be long?" Freya asked. "Only I want to find my bedroom so I can shower and unpack properly."

"Go ahead," I said to her and Ruby.

"See you at dinner," Ruby said, and Freya nodded.

They left me alone, and I stared at the sheets, willing something to leap out at me.

I sensed someone behind me and turned to find Conrad there.

He leaned over me so he could see the pages. "Cookery," he said. "What else?"

I swallowed, suddenly too warm.

"I was thinking about orienteering," I said, "but I can't find the sheet."

"Let me see."

Conrad moved in front of me. I heard him shuffling the papers, then he held one up and turned back to face me.

"It's here," he said. "No sign-ups. That's awkward for me – I'm supposed to be popular."

"You're running orienteering?" I asked, my pen hovering over the sheet

He nodded. "It's not something I talk about online, but I'm pretty good at reading maps. And I quite like getting lost."

I signed up, telling myself I'd been planning to do it *before* I knew Conrad was running the course.

"I'm also doing forest bathing," Conrad said. "If you want to save me from the embarrassment of no one wanting to do that too?"

"What is it?"

"We go into the woods, and we use our senses to really take it in. It sounds like hippy nonsense, I know, but it's a big part of Japanese wellbeing culture. My aunt got me into it. I ... I have pretty bad anxiety sometimes. Whenever I get stressed, I picture the forest and remember how it looked and smelled and sounded. It helps. But if you're not interested, I get it. We'd be stuck in the woods together for hours – alone, by the looks of it. Orienteering is more than enough time with me, right?"

"Wouldn't it be weird to have two sessions just the two of us?" I asked.

Conrad gave a slow smile. "Actually, I think it would be perfect."

I signed my name on the sheet, trying to hide my blushing face.

CHAPTER 4

"What do you mean there isn't a room for me?"
I asked.

I stared at the man in white who was standing like a guard on the landing by the attic. It was where we were all supposed to be staying.

"All the rooms have been allocated. There's no Ivy Finch on my list," he repeated. "I'm sorry."

Panic began to bubble in my chest. "Where's my case, then? Where am I supposed to sleep?"

The man gave me a sympathetic smile. "You'll need to check with Miss Nilsson. She'll be in her office, just off the main hall."

I spun round and headed back down the stairs.

Dagmar's office was marked with her name on a small gold sign. I knocked on the door, my heart pounding.

"Come in," she called.

Dagmar was sitting behind a large desk that was so shiny I could see her reflection in it.

"Ivy. How can I help?" Dagmar said, closing her laptop and looking at me.

"Apparently, I'm not on the room list," I said.

Dagmar nodded. "Yes, that's right. You see, we only planned to have twelve participants at first. But after I read your application, I decided to make an exception for you. I didn't think it was fair to make you share with someone, so I put you in one of the family guest bedrooms. I'm sorry you won't be with the others. But the family rooms do have private bathrooms, so hopefully that will make up for it. Is that OK?" Dagmar said.

I managed a nod. A room in the main part of the house with its own bathroom? Everyone who didn't already hate me would after this.

Dagmar stood and smoothed down her white skirt.

"I'll show you," she said. "You'll soon feel at home."

I followed her out of the office and across the hallway to the large staircase on the left-hand side. It was blocked by a thick red rope, but Dagmar unhooked it and let me pass, then put it back, letting everyone else know this area was off-limits.

At the top of the stairs, Dagmar opened a door marked *Private*, which led into a long corridor. We passed three other doors before Dagmar stopped and opened one.

"You'll be in here," she said. "The blue room."

I stepped inside, relieved to see my suitcase standing by a large wardrobe.

The room was *very* blue, with wallpaper in a silvery pattern on a pale blue background. The bedspread was a darker blue, covering a wooden double bed. On each side were two matching wooden tables – both had lamps, and the one on the left had an old-fashioned alarm clock on it, ticking softly. In one corner was the wardrobe and a chest of drawers, and in the other a desk and chair. It was nice, even if it smelled stale, as if no one had slept in here in a while.

"The bathroom is in here." Dagmar walked to a door opposite the bed and opened it. I caught a flash of blue tiles. "There are fresh towels in the cupboard. You should have everything you need, but of course ask if you don't." Dagmar smiled. "I'll leave you to freshen up. Dinner is in an hour."

She nodded at the alarm clock by the bed and then left, closing the door behind her.

It was quiet. I'd never been anywhere so quiet before. If it weren't for the ticking of the clock, there would be no sound at all. I crossed the room and looked out of the window. It seemed like my room was at the back of the house, or maybe the side, because it faced the woods that surrounded Chalmers Hall.

I spent the hour before dinner unpacking and peeping into the drawers and cupboards. It reminded me of being in one of my favourite horror games – exploring the rooms in an old house to see if there was anything I could pick up for my inventory before I had to go outside and fight the monsters. But I didn't find anything – only a dead spider at the back of the desk drawer. There were no monsters at the Ash Tree Foundation.

"I can't believe you're sleeping in the main part of the house while we suffer in the attic," Ruby said at dinner later. "So unfair."

"What's it like?" Freya asked, sitting beside me.

"It's nice," I replied. "I mean, I've only seen my room so far. I feel like I shouldn't snoop."

"You absolutely should," Ruby said, spearing a roast potato with her fork. "You owe it to us to snoop."

We were sitting at a table in the dining room next to the ballroom. Ruby, Freya and I were at the far end, furthest from where Conrad and Dagmar sat at a table alone. Staff in white clothes moved around, bringing things to the buffet and clearing the empty dishes away.

"They're a bit cult-y," Freya said when a silent girl in a white dress put down another dish of roast chicken. "Why do they wear white? It's not very practical."

"A bigger mystery is why Conrad O'Connell can't stop staring at Ivy," Ruby said, nodding in Conrad's direction.

I looked up and caught Conrad's eye.

He gave me a soft smile.

Ruby gasped. "Ivy, I think he's into you."

I turned scarlet. "No, he isn't," I said, turning away.

When I dared to glance back, Conrad was still looking at me.

*

Orienteering was my first session, the next morning after breakfast.

I was waiting for Conrad in the hallway outside Dagmar's office. Ruby and Freya had gone to the sewing session in the conservatory. I'd slept really well in the blue room, better than everyone in the attic. Apparently, the walls up there were really thin, and every time someone snored, or turned over and made the bed creak, it woke everyone up.

"Hi," Conrad said, appearing from inside Dagmar's office and making me jump. He was wearing a waxy-looking green jacket and hiking boots, and had a large rucksack on his back.

"Hello," I said, my stomach suddenly jittery.

Conrad looked me up and down and frowned. "Are they the only shoes you have?" he said, nodding at my trainers. "What size are you?"

"Five," I said. "What's wrong with them?"

He chewed his lip. "Give me a second." He disappeared into Dagmar's office again and came back out with a pair of black hiking boots in his hands. They were like the ones he had on. Conrad held them out to me.

"They're new, don't worry," he added when I didn't take them. "Dagmar says you can have them. She hates hiking."

"I'll be OK like this," I said. "It's not like we're climbing a mountain, is it?"

"No, but it's muddy in the woods. Your trainers will get trashed. It doesn't matter if the walking boots get messy – that's what they're for. Honestly, it's fine. Take them."

I didn't want to look ungrateful or stubborn, so I did. I took my trainers off, feeling eternally grateful my socks didn't have holes, and left them in a hidden closet Conrad opened in the wood panelling by the door.

"Let's go orienteer ourselves," he said.

I felt eyes on me as we left the house. I turned to see Ruby, Freya and some of the others sitting in the conservatory with their sewing stuff in their hands. They were all staring at me and Conrad. Ruby gave me a thumbs-up, and I flashed her a grin.

We walked down the gravel driveway and turned right into the woods that surrounded Chalmers Hall.

"How big is this place?" I asked as we walked. Conrad was in front, me just behind.

"Four hundred acres, if you include both of the woods, the tennis courts, the ponds and the old folly. We're heading to Boar Woods. Don't worry, there are no boar in there these days. The birdwatching and the photography are happening in Chalmers Woods. Boar Woods is a bit wilder, which is what we want."

"What's a folly?" I asked him.

"It's a rich-person thing. People who built big houses like Chalmers Hall would sometimes build a kind of miniature tower or castle in the grounds, called a folly. The one here was built in

Victorian times, at the same time as the hall, but the builders made it look like a medieval castle."

"Why?" I asked.

"Because they could," Conrad said. "They're mostly for decoration, but sometimes they'd have picnics or parties in them. I guess if you're out walking, then it's something fun to come across."

"Is it far?"

Conrad shook his head. "No, it's just over there." He pointed to the left. "By the lake. But we can't go there. It's not safe," he added before I could ask why not. "It's a ruin. It could collapse any time."

I was disappointed. Exploring ruins was one of my favourite things to do in some of the games I played. It would have been nice to see some in real life.

We walked on for a while and didn't see a single other person. I wondered what my mothers would say if they knew I was in the woods alone with a boy I'd only just met. They wouldn't be happy, I decided. But it was their idea for me to come here. And no one else seemed worried.

"You OK?" Conrad turned back to ask me.

"Yes. I'm great."

The path was less well worn here, and the gaps between the trees were smaller. It was darker and smelled greener somehow. I knew without Conrad needing to tell me that we'd entered Boar Woods.

CHAPTER 5

It felt like hours had passed by the time Conrad finally stopped and perched on a rotting log. He pulled the rucksack from his back and took out two bottles of water, handing one to me. The water tasted good: cold and clean. I was thirstier than I'd realised.

"All right," he said as he put the cap back on his bottle. "So, this isn't true orienteering because there aren't any proper orienteering maps of the grounds. I'm making one at the moment." His cheeks flushed pink. "So, we're going to use a normal map and a compass to practise instead. You're going to guide us to a spot we pick on the map. We'll have lunch there, and then you can map our route home."

"I don't know how to do any of that," I said.

"It's easy. I'll show you." He patted the spot next to him.

As I sat down, Conrad reached into his bag again and took out a large compass and a paper map, which he unfolded across both of our knees. His leg was touching mine, and even in our jeans I could feel how warm he was. It made it hard to concentrate.

"We're here," he said, pointing to a spot on a trail marked by dashes. "The path splits up there." He pointed ahead. "And I think it'd be nice to have lunch at the wishing well." He pointed to a tiny cross on the map.

Then he handed me the compass. "Can you figure out which direction we need to go in when the path forks?"

"I'm really bad at this," I said. "It's why I wanted to do the course. Whenever I play *Zelda*, I can't keep hold of the directions in my head. It's like my brain can't translate the map into the actual game, and I end up running around with no idea where I'm going."

"I promise by the time you go home you'll be able to do it," Conrad said. Then he pulled a face. "I've never played *Zelda*."

"Never?" I said, my jaw dropping. "Any of them?"

He shook his head.

"I think you'd like it," I said. "They're my all-time favourite games. There's a lot of cooking and stuff like this." I gestured to the woods. "Loads of exploring ruins and follies too. You don't even have to do the quests if you don't want to. You can just ride horses and make potions and fight monsters."

"Sounds fun," Conrad said with a smile, and held the compass out to me. "Here. Find north," he said.

I knew how to do that at least.

"There," I said, pointing behind us, in the direction we'd come from.

"Good. Which way do we need to go to get to the wishing well?"

I stared at the map and the compass, then took the map from him and laid it on the ground. I turned it until the path we'd followed was behind us.

"That way," I said, pointing up and to the right, then looked at the compass again. "Erm ... south-west when the path forks?"

Conrad beamed. "Exactly! I knew you could do it. Let's go, Zelda."

I was about to correct him, to tell him that Link was the character you played in the *Zelda* games, not Zelda, but he looked so happy. I didn't want to make him feel bad.

I liked him, I realised. I was starting to *really* like him.

*

We sat on the side of the wishing well and ate cheese sandwiches and crisps that Conrad had packed. The well was covered in ivy and looked like something that would be in *Zelda* – the kind of thing a Great Fairy would be living in. Someone had fitted a safety grate over the top so you couldn't fall in, but I managed to drop a stone into one of the gaps, and I didn't hear it hit the bottom.

Conrad packed our litter away when we'd finished eating, then reached up and plucked a leaf from the ivy.

"Like your name," Conrad said, twining some around his fingers. "It's pretty. Like ..." He stopped and turned away.

I felt myself burn so red I was surprised I didn't burst into flames.

He let me navigate on the way back, and we didn't get lost. I knew that was mainly because there were paths to follow – it wasn't as if we were in the wilderness. But it still felt good to look at the map and the compass and see how they worked together. I liked knowing that even if there weren't paths, I could figure it out, more or less.

"Maybe one day I won't have to flip the map around to use it," I said as we tramped up the gravel driveway back to the main house. "Here." I held the map and compass out to him.

"Keep them. You can practise with them if you want," Conrad said.

"Thanks."

He bent to take his hiking boots off, tucking them back in the hidden cupboard and hanging his coat on the hooks below a shelf full of torches.

I carefully took Dagmar's boots off too and put them next to his.

"What are—" Conrad began, but he stopped as Dagmar came out of her office.

"There you are," she said. "I need you."

Conrad turned to me. "See you later," he said, following his aunt.

I stared after him for a moment, then headed up to my room for a shower.

*

Ruby and Freya waited for me in the main hall before we went to dinner that night.

"Everyone hates you," Ruby said. "Half our sewing class were begging to switch to orienteering."

"They all said they didn't even see the orienteering sheet and it wasn't fair," Freya added.

I remembered how I hadn't been able to find it either until Conrad did. I'd got really lucky.

"Are they allowed to swap?" I asked.

Ruby and Freya shook their heads. "Nope. So it looks like you get the Boy Wonder all to yourself," Freya said.

I hesitated. "And for forest bathing too," I admitted. "He's running that. I was the only person who signed up."

Freya whistled.

"Girl, you're going to get murdered in your fancy bed," Ruby said. She linked an arm with mine and pulled me into the dining room.

As we sat down, two girls came over to us – the red-haired one and her friend who'd sat in front of us the day before and talked about whether Conrad would be leading birdwatching.

"Hi, Ivy. Can we sit here?" the red-haired one said. "I'm Grace and this is Bella." She pointed at her friend.

"There are only four seats," Ruby pointed out.

"We can all fit if we squash up a bit. You can move if you're uncomfortable," Bella said.

Ruby's jaw dropped.

"Wait a second," Freya said. "Do you want to sit with Ivy because you're interested in her or because you want to see if she can get you in with Conrad?"

Grace glared at Freya.

"Who even are you?" Grace said. "We were talking to Ivy."

The way she looked at Freya made my blood boil. "Actually, the spare seat is taken," I said.

"Oh really? By who?" Bella asked.

"Me," said a voice.

As if by magic, Conrad had appeared at our table.

"Thanks for holding my seat, Ivy," he said. "Sorry I took so long."

He pulled out the chair and sat down, then turned to Grace and Bella. "I think there's room over there," he said, pointing to an empty table. "And it's nearer the buffet too. Enjoy your dinner," he added, then turned his back on them.

Grace opened her mouth like she wanted to protest, then rushed away, Bella trailing after her.

"Are you all right?" Conrad asked me.

"I'm fine. Let me introduce you," I said. "This is Conrad, but you already knew that. Conrad, this is Ruby and Freya."

"Hi, Ruby," Conrad said to Ruby. He didn't even look at Freya.

I saw Freya's cheeks darken as blood rushed to them, and a second later she stood up and left the dining room.

Ruby and I stared after her.

"I'm going to make sure she's OK," Ruby said, giving Conrad a strange look.

Then she was gone too, and we were alone.

"What was all that about?" I asked Conrad.

He pulled a face I couldn't interpret and said, "I know Freya. Sort of."

"Right." I remembered that Freya said she and Conrad had starting posting about the environment at the same time.

Conrad frowned at me. "Did she tell you what she did to end up here?" he asked.

I shook my head. "She just said she was an eco-influencer. Like you."

"I shouldn't say this," Conrad whispered, leaning forward. "But ... be careful of her."

"What do you mean?" I asked.

"I can't say any more than that. Just promise me you'll be on your guard around Freya. Not everyone here is like you, Ivy. Some of them *are* the people who did the bad thing, not the victims. Promise you'll take care."

Conrad's eyes fixed on mine, and for a second I thought he was going to take my hand.

"I promise," I said.

He smiled and sat back in his chair. "Good. Let's go and see what's on the menu."

CHAPTER 6

Ruby and Freya didn't come back to dinner, and no one else interrupted Conrad and me. We talked so much I didn't notice everyone else had left the dining room. The staff were clearing up when one of them came over to us.

"So sorry to interrupt, Mr O'Connell," the man in white said. "Your aunt is looking for you."

"Right," Conrad said, and stood up at once. "I'd better go. I'll see you tomorrow."

"There's a film playing in the ballroom, Miss," the man in white said to me as Conrad left. "I think that's where all the others are. It should be just starting."

He clearly wanted me out of the dining room.

"Great. Thanks," I said, standing and reaching for my tray.

"I'll see to that, Miss," he replied, taking it from me and leaving me with no choice but to go.

I got to the entrance of the ballroom and saw the trailers were playing on a huge screen – someone had hooked up a projector. I scanned the room for Ruby and Freya but couldn't find them. I didn't want to go in there alone.

I left, about to head up to the blue room to practise with the map and compass Conrad had given me, but I paused, an idea forming.

Conrad had said the folly was dangerous, but my idea wasn't to go inside it. I could just find it and look at it from a distance. It would be a good chance to practise using the compass and the map, and it would be so cool to see real-life ruins. There was never going to be a better opportunity than just now while everyone else was busy.

I ran up to the blue room and opened the map on the bed. Conrad had said the folly was by the lake, which I found on the map easily, just a short walk away. If I turned left out of the front door and followed the road, I'd soon reach the track that would take me to the lake. I could walk around the edge of that to find the folly – it wasn't marked on the map for some reason.

I crept back down to the hall, pausing at the bottom of the stairs. The door to Dagmar's office was closed, and I could hear the film playing faintly, deeper in the house. I tiptoed over to the hidden cupboard and took a torch from the shelf above the coats as quietly as I could. I debated changing into the walking shoes but decided I'd be fine in my trainers because I wasn't going into the woods.

Then I crept out into the night.

*

It was eerie to be outside in the dark, surrounded by so many trees. It was quiet and still, so different to where I lived. The moon was full above me, making everything bright and silvery. I could see how the road turned into the woods just a little way ahead. Once I got round the bend, the trees blocked Chalmers Hall from view, showing me only the odd glimmer of light between their leaves.

I walked for a bit longer before I risked turning the torch on, and then squealed with surprise as a rabbit dashed across the road in front of me. I laughed at myself for being freaked out by a bunny, then cried out again when an owl hooted right above my head.

Suddenly, coming out in the dark alone didn't feel like such a clever idea. No one knew where I was, and I didn't have my phone to call for help if something went wrong. I was just about to turn back when I saw a pile of stones reaching up to my waist on the opposite side of the road, with something white on top of them. It looked so strange that I went over to it.

As I got closer, I saw the white thing was a small skull with long canine teeth. I had no idea what kind of animal it belonged to. My hand was halfway to my pocket to get my phone to look it up when I remembered I didn't have it. I wasn't freaked out by the skull, because this was the countryside, and it was clean and clearly old. But I did wonder who had left it here, and why. Was it a warning? A joke? If this was a game, it would mean something important. I cast the torch about, grinning when I spotted a track leading into the woods.

The skull was a signpost. It meant there was danger this way for those bold enough to dare follow it.

Well, I already knew the ruins were dangerous. And I knew from gaming that the places you were warned away from always had the best rewards.

I gave the skull a nod of respect as I passed, glad no one could see me, and then turned onto the track.

The path was narrow but clear. I'd expected it to be overgrown because the folly was off-limits, but it seemed like the gardeners kept it tidy anyway. I walked and walked, listening carefully, the light of the torch bouncing on the path in front of me. I spotted the lake beyond the trees before I reached it, the water glittering in the light from the moon.

And there was the folly.

As soon as I broke out onto the shore of the lake, I saw it on my left. The folly looked exactly like a miniature castle, with battlements on the top and large arched windows that had no glass in but were filled with a soft, golden, flickering light.

Someone was in the folly.

I hesitated, not sure what to do.

Conrad had seemed so sure it was out of bounds, but someone was in there right now with a fire lit or candles burning. Maybe they didn't know the folly was in danger of falling down at any second. If I didn't warn them and something happened to them, I'd never forgive myself. But what if they were criminals, smugglers or drug barons or something and I interrupted them?

I shivered, because that would go very badly for me, especially without a phone to call for help. It would be very easy to make one girl disappear, and no one would realise I was missing until the next day.

There was also the fact I wasn't supposed to be out here at all.

I'd sneak over, I decided. See what was going on without letting them know I was there, then I'd make a decision about what to do next.

I turned the torch off and made my way slowly to the folly, sticking close to the edge of the woods. As I got closer, I heard a low hum, but it wasn't until I was right outside that I realised the hum was voices coming from *inside* the folly. There was no one guarding the entrance, so I moved closer. My knees turned to jelly and the torch shook in my hand as I peered around the stone door frame into the folly.

A group of people stood around inside, all wearing white, just like the staff at Chalmers Hall. Then I realised it *was* the staff from Chalmers Hall. At the centre of it all were Dagmar and Conrad.

Dagmar was talking with excitement. I couldn't make out the words, but I could see her hands moving, while Conrad and the people in white nodded.

What were they doing? What was this place? Why was Conrad there when he'd told me it was too dangerous?

I leaned around a little more to try to get a better look ...

And that was the moment Conrad stared right at me.

His eyes locked on to mine, and for a moment I couldn't move, pinned in place under the strength of his gaze.

Then Conrad's attention flicked to Dagmar, his eyes widening as she started to turn around.

Conrad said something and tugged her hand, and that was all I needed.

I burst away, racing back the way I'd come, leaving the torch off, terrified at any moment I'd hear footsteps behind me, hunting me down.

But I made it back to Chalmers Hall without being caught. I threw myself inside, panting, a stitch in my side from running. I could hear the film still playing in the ballroom, so I chucked the torch back in the cupboard, smoothed down my hair and then sneaked into the back of the ballroom. I sat in a seat in the corner and tried to slow my heart down, my mind whirring with everything I'd seen. Had Conrad told his aunt I'd been there? Were they on their way back here right now to call my parents and throw me out?

When the film ended ten minutes later and the lights came up, I clapped with everyone else.

"Ivy!" Grace said when she turned around and saw me. "I didn't know you were here! You should have come and sat with us."

"I got here late, and I didn't want to be the person who ruined the show," I said, my voice shaking a little.

"What did you think of the film?" asked Bella, Grace's friend.

"To be honest, I kind of fell asleep," I lied. "I walked a lot today, and I guess I'm not used to it."

"Oh my god, that's right – you had orienteering alone with Conrad," Grace said. "What was that like?"

I faked a yawn, standing up. "It was fine, but I'm so tired now." I added another yawn. "I think I'd better get to bed. Goodnight!" I said, then walked away as fast as I could.

I climbed the stairs to the blue room, my head spinning as I tried to process everything I'd seen at the folly. What had they been doing there?

When I opened the door to my bedroom, Dagmar Nilsson was sitting on my bed.

CHAPTER 7

"I think we need to talk, Ivy, don't you?" Dagmar said, patting the spot on the bed beside her.

I couldn't move, hovering in the doorway.

"I'm sorry," I said.

"You're not in any trouble," Dagmar replied. "The opposite, in fact. Please, Ivy. Close the door and come and sit down."

I shut the door as instructed and perched next to her on the bed.

"I didn't really see anything ..." I began, stopping when Dagmar laughed.

"What was there to see?" she said. "A group of work colleagues having a chat. But I can understand why coming across us at night might have looked spooky." She paused, and her smile dropped. "What were you doing out there?" Dagmar asked.

"I wanted to see the folly," I admitted. "Conrad told me it was off-limits because it was dangerous. I didn't want to go in – just to see it. I thought if I sneaked out, no one would know."

There was no point in lying. I'd left the open map on my bed. She must have seen it when she came in.

Dagmar nodded. "The folly is perfectly safe. I started the white lie about it being dangerous to keep people away. You see, it's where we're doing our most important work, our *real* work, and it's vital that it stays a secret until we're ready to share it."

"I'm sorry," I said, feeling ashamed. "I didn't know."

"You were curious," Dagmar said. "It's a good quality to be curious."

"Are you going to send me home?"

I didn't think I could face my parents' disappointment. But to my surprise, Dagmar laughed again.

"We're not going to send you home, Ivy. No, I think perhaps you're exactly what we've been looking for."

I shook my head. "I don't understand."

Dagmar leaned towards me. "What I'm about to tell you is extremely confidential. You can't tell anyone. You must promise."

I thought about Ruby and Freya, and felt a twinge of guilt. I'd only just met them, but I liked them.

Then I reasoned that they had gone off and left me at dinner, so maybe they didn't care about me. They'd clearly bonded during sewing, while I was out with Conrad. If I was honest with myself, I probably should be kicked out of the I Hate Conrad O'Connell Club anyway as I didn't hate him at all. They didn't need a third wheel making everything awkward.

"I promise I won't say anything," I said. "You can trust me."

"I really hope so, Ivy," Dagmar said. "You know, I suspected it would be you from your records. I had a really strong feeling. Conrad did too. It's why we made room for you despite being full. I don't like to brag, but one of my talents is spotting potential, and I knew the second I read your application that you had potential."

"What does that mean? Potential for what?" I asked.

Dagmar took a deep breath. "The Ash Tree Foundation is a little bit more than just a camp for teenagers who need a digital detox. We have a much bigger purpose. For most of the people here, it really is just a four-week opportunity for them to reset their relationship with technology. But for some people – people like you – it can be so much more. For you, Ivy, this could be the beginning of your entire future."

Goosebumps rose on my skin even though the room was warm.

"How?" I asked, almost whispering.

Dagmar's face shone with pride as she spoke. "We believe the reason people need to take breaks from technology is because they don't have a good relationship with it. That's not their fault, because for hundreds and thousands of years we had basic tools we developed as a community. Then suddenly, in the last few decades, we've had an endless amount of new tools and gadgets developed by the very rich, which only the very rich can access fully. We have to keep buying the new technology and getting the updates or we can't participate in society any more. You must have a smartphone to order food in a restaurant, or log into your bank, or communicate with your loved ones. No wonder some people become addicted and dependent." Dagmar laughed. "But what we want to do at the Foundation is create a platform that makes things truly equal, so no one is left behind. Do you know what *symbiotic* means?"

I shook my head.

"It means when two species develop a close and long-term relationship with each other that helps them both survive. To thrive even. That's what we want to accomplish here. All people and a universal technology working together in harmony."

"Do we need that?" I asked before I could stop myself.

"I think so," Dagmar replied, her expression serious. "Especially normal people like us. We're already at the mercy of a changing planet – my nephew frightens me every day with his updates about the climate disaster and heatwaves and floods. We're going to need real resources to help us deal with that, and soon. We at the Foundation believe that technology, in the right hands, can help us with that. And, let's be honest, the billionaire tech bros of Silicon Valley aren't going to stop churning out new products any time soon, so there has to be something to balance that, don't you think? Something that really does benefit humankind, not just shareholders."

I nodded. It did make sense. It felt like every morning at home my parents would talk about something they'd seen in the news where technology was making things worse. AI home assistants encouraging people to commit crimes, people using apps to phish details and ruin lives ... If the Foundation really was trying to help counter what the big corporations were doing, that would be amazing.

"But it has to be a secret until it's ready," Dagmar said. "If they find out we're trying to stop them, they'll use their money and their big fancy lawyers to come after us and try to steal our work. That's why the public-facing side of the Foundation is only the tech-detox camp. The real work is something only a few people know about. Including you now, Ivy."

"What is the work?" I asked.

"It will be easier to show you than to explain," Dagmar said. "But that will mean you'll have to stop attending the activity sessions. Which ones are you doing?"

"Cooking," I said. "Forest bathing and orienteering are just me and Conrad anyway."

"Perfect," Dagmar said. "I can come up with a reason why you can't attend cooking any more."

"Will I still be here, at Chalmers Hall?" I asked.

"Oh yes. You'll still see the others at mealtimes. And Conrad, if you want."

My skin started to heat up, and I cleared my throat, trying to force the blush down.

"Do I need to do anything?" I asked. "Do my parents need to sign anything?"

Dagmar shook her head. "No. They already gave you permission to take part in the activities hosted by the Foundation, and the new task you'll be doing comes under that umbrella."

"OK," I said, a tingle of excitement running through me. "Then I'm in."

Dagmar beamed at me, showing twin rows of perfect white teeth. "I'm so pleased. Your gaming skills make you perfect for this. We couldn't believe our luck when your application came in. Conrad will be delighted you're on board too."

My cheeks burned again.

Dagmar rose and smoothed her skirt down. "Conrad will show you what we're really doing here after breakfast. I can't tell you how happy you've made me, Ivy. The work you're going to do will change lives. Now, get some sleep and come to my office in the morning, bright and early. OK?"

"OK," I said.

Dagmar gave me another huge smile and then left. I threw myself back onto the bed, rolling over and squealing into the pillows.

I can't believe this is happening, I thought as I rolled onto my back and pulled a pillow to my chest, hugging it to me. When I'd found Dagmar sitting on my bed, I'd thought I was done for – that my mom was probably already in the car on the way to take me home. But instead I was going to help the Foundation with their real work.

I thought of Ruby and Freya, and another worm of guilt wriggled in my belly, but I forced it to still. It sounded like what I'd be doing with Dagmar would be really helpful to people like them, who needed to come on tech detoxes. The best way for me to be a real friend to them would be helping the Foundation fight back against what all the big tech corporations were doing.

And it would make my mom and my mum proud too. They were always saying I should think about the future and get more involved with things, and that was exactly what I was doing. Dagmar had said that it was actually my gaming experience that made me perfect to help the Foundation.

Maybe I had been getting ready for the future all along.

CHAPTER 8

Conrad was waiting for me outside Dagmar's office early the next morning.

"Dagmar told me she spoke to you. I'm so happy you're joining us," he said as we walked towards the dining hall.

"I was worried you'd be angry because I sneaked out to the folly," I admitted. "When you saw me, I thought my heart was going to stop."

Conrad laughed. "Not angry at all. Actually, I can say now that telling you it was off-limits was a test – to see if you'd go along with it. We needed to know if you had what it takes to break the rules sometimes. It's important to the Foundation that we recruit people who can think for themselves."

"I can think for myself," I said.

Inside the dining hall, the staff were still setting up.

"You're a little early for food, I'm afraid, Mr O'Connell," one of the staff in white said.

"That's all right – we're good with coffee for now," Conrad said. I nodded as he poured a cup for each of us.

We sat at the same table we'd been at the night before.

"Your aunt is really something," I said.

"She's amazing. Way better than my uncle's first wife."

"She's your aunt through marriage?" I said.

Conrad nodded. "My uncle married her five years ago. She's changed his whole life. She's a lot younger than him, but he needed someone fresh and full of energy. He owned a business in technology solutions, and he sold it for ... well, a lot of money. But after that he just drifted around, not really doing anything. Then he met Dagmar at a conference, and they fell in love. She convinced him to buy this place and let her set up the Ash Tree Foundation. She really wants to make a difference."

"Where's your uncle now?" I asked.

"He's at home in London. He doesn't come here much. He had a bit of a run-in with the locals because he tried to fence off Boar Woods and the pond, and he hasn't been back since. He only did it to protect the Foundation's real work, but Dagmar got worried about the attention, so she made him take the fence down. What about your family?" Conrad asked.

"It's just me and my mothers."

"You have two mums?"

I nodded. "Yeah. My mom and my mum."

"Is one of them American?" Conrad asked.

"No. But neither of them wanted to be called 'mother' or 'mama', so they settled on 'mom' and 'mum'. Plus, my mom is from Birmingham, and they say mom there, like in America."

"What's it like, having two mums, if it's not rude to ask?" Conrad said.

"Not rude at all." I tried to think of a way to explain it. "Sometimes it's great, but other times it's intense. To be honest, I don't know anything else."

"I only have a mum," Conrad said. "My dad left when I was a baby."

"I bet he regrets it now you're an internet superstar," I said. Then something occurred to me. "Wait, you lied to me. You said you were anti-tech, but you can't be if you're involved with the Foundation's real work."

"I never said I was anti-tech, just that it's what I'm known for," Conrad said. "I did admit to being a fake. I couldn't tell you the whole truth at the time."

I nodded. I supposed it made sense, to help keep the Foundation's cover.

"Are you still uploading videos while you're here?" I asked. "Are you even allowed to be offline?"

Conrad made a huffing sound. "Not really. My sponsors don't like it. I pre-filmed a bunch of content to upload. And I still have my phone if I need to make anything in a hurry," he said. "But you can't tell the others. Especially Freya."

I mimed zipping my mouth shut.

"You really don't like her, do you?" I asked.

Conrad pulled a face, then looked around us.

"This is confidential, but Freya did some seriously bad things. She really hurt a friend of mine," he said in a whisper. "We have a policy that means everyone gets a clean slate as soon as they arrive, but you're not one of them any more, you're one of us, so I guess it's OK to tell you about her."

Conrad paused. "Freya is here because she was jealous of this other girl, and she tried to ruin her life. They'd been best friends when they were kids, but they'd grown apart, and afterwards Hye-jin got pretty famous—"

"Do you mean Kim Hye-jin?" I interrupted. Even I'd heard of her – she was a guest presenter on a TV show my parents loved. "My mom is always telling me I should go outside and be more like Hye-jin."

Conrad gave a bitter laugh.

"Funny, because that was exactly Freya's problem," he said. "She wanted to be so much like Hye-jin that she tried to steal her life. Freya set up fake social-media profiles and then committed crimes and made it look like Hye-jin had done it. She was almost arrested. All because of Freya."

CHAPTER 9

"Oh my god," I said.

I couldn't believe what Conrad was telling me. Freya seemed nice, if a little quiet. I knew you couldn't really tell what someone was like from how they looked, but she didn't seem like a criminal mastermind.

Conrad continued, "Freya wanted so badly to be popular that she'd do anything. It was really bad. I got dragged into it too."

My eyes widened. "How?"

"I reposted something Hye-jin put up. We posted the same kind of thing, both trying to raise awareness about the climate crisis, and suddenly there were all these rumours we were dating … I'm pretty sure Freya started them to try to make my fans hate Hye-jin and go after her. Freya's … bad news."

I took a sip of my coffee. "Wow. I had no idea."

"I didn't want her here, but my aunt said she was exactly the sort of person who needed our help most of all." He shook his head.

"What about Ruby?" I asked. "Is she … dangerous?"

"She's fine. She got into a situation with a guy she met on an app, and he ended up stalking her." Conrad shrugged. "Anyway, Ruby's a bit naive, but not evil. Not that I'm saying Freya is evil," he added quickly. "Just … like you said, dangerous. But hopefully being here will help her. Dagmar really believes it will."

"Huh." I breathed out slowly. "So you know about me, then? Getting sucked in by someone online."

Conrad looked shy. "Yes, but we could see you were different. I read what happened, and it sounds like you were just unlucky. You did everything you could to stay safe – you looked the guy up and did the research, and when it went bad, you saved yourself. That's really impressive."

"Thanks," I said.

"It's that kind of thinking that we need at the Foundation. People who are smart and can make smart choices based on real evidence. And can think for themselves. I said that already. Most people don't think for themselves at all."

"And that's how the tech companies get them," I added. "Because they don't stop and think about what's really going on."

"Exactly," Conrad replied. "I think breakfast is served."

Suddenly, I was starving. Dinner last night felt like days ago. By the time the others began to arrive, Conrad and I were on our second platefuls of toast and eggs and our third coffees.

I knew that Freya and Ruby had arrived before I saw them. Conrad had stiffened, then looked down at his plate.

To my total shock, a few moments later they joined us, Freya trailing after Ruby.

"Mind if we sit here?" Ruby said, plonking herself down.

Freya hovered behind her.

"Not at all," Conrad said, looking up and giving her a wide smile. "Please, sit down, Freya."

She sat in the seat opposite him and began pushing her cereal around with her spoon.

"Sorry we ditched you last night," Ruby said to me. "Did you see the film?"

"Yeah. But I fell asleep just after it started. Didn't wake up until everyone clapped at the end," I said. "Must have been all the walking during orienteering."

"What about you?" Ruby asked Conrad.

"I had things to do."

"And you're forest bathing today, right?" Ruby said.

"Yes," I said. "What are you doing?"

"Nothing. Freya is swimming, but I didn't take a third option because nothing appealed."

"What about creative writing?" I asked. "I thought you wanted to work on a script."

Ruby shook her head. "I can do that anywhere. So, I was thinking ... I could sign up for forest bathing too as there's no one else doing it but Ivy."

"No swapping," Conrad snapped. "Sorry."

"It's not a swap," Ruby insisted. "I'm not signed up for anything else during this time."

"It's too late," Conrad said. "We've already got everything set up."

Ruby gave a laugh. "Like what? The woods? I don't think the trees will mind if there's an extra person you didn't warn them about."

"It's a no," Conrad said, standing up so fast his chair nearly toppled over. "Sorry. Come on, Ivy. We have to go."

Ruby and Freya gave each other a long, meaningful look.

I felt bad about how rude he was being, even as I understood Conrad couldn't let Ruby join us because we weren't really going forest bathing. But when I saw Ruby and Freya exchange that knowing secret look, my heart hardened. I was right – they had already bonded, and I refused to be the third wheel.

"See you later," I said, leaving my tray at the table like Conrad had and following him out.

Like the day before, we went to the hidden cupboard and changed our shoes, pulling outdoor jackets on.

"We don't want to look suspicious," Conrad said as he swung his rucksack onto his shoulders. "So we'll head towards the woods and then follow the track down to the folly. Is that how you got there?"

I nodded. "I saw a little skull sitting on top of a pile of rocks by the entrance. It reminded me of something from a game – you have to look for the thing that doesn't fit in sometimes and it leads you to hidden treasure or a side quest or something."

Conrad beamed. "Exactly! I put that there for you! I hoped you'd spot it and understand it was a sign."

I smiled back.

The skull wasn't there any more and nor was the pile of stones. Conrad explained that he'd taken them away now I'd passed the test and found the folly. He didn't want anyone else getting curious. We walked in single file down to the lake, then turned towards the small castle-like building.

It was less imposing in the daylight. I could see that it was more modern than it had looked in the dark – clearly a copy of an old castle, not a real one from centuries ago.

My heart began to beat faster as we approached it. I was excited and nervous about what I'd find inside. Some fear crept in too. What if I wasn't what they wanted me to be? What if I let them down?

There was no one inside the folly, and it was empty of everything except a giant stone that looked like an old tomb at the far end.

To my surprise, Conrad walked over to it.

He felt around under the rim, and a second later I heard a soft grating noise as the lid of the tomb swung around.

"Cool," I breathed as I spotted the staircase that led down underneath the folly.

"Welcome to the real Foundation," Conrad said. He climbed over the side of the fake tomb and onto the stairs.

He held out a hand for me, and I took it, following him down a little way. Then he pressed a button on a control panel at the side. For a moment, I panicked as the tomb lid began to swing back into place, terrified we'd be trapped in the dark. But just before it closed, a series of electric lights came on, showing that the stairs led down to a thick metal door.

"You OK?" Conrad asked, and I nodded.

We walked down the stairs hand in hand.

At the bottom, Connor flipped open another control panel and tapped in a series of numbers. The door opened with a faint hiss, and the lights on the stairs switched off.

"After you," Conrad said, and pushed the door wide.

I walked into the heart of the Foundation.

CHAPTER 10

It was a gamer's paradise. It was my dream come true. The best thing I'd ever seen.

Three walls were completely covered by massive screens, and in front of them were fully kitted-out gaming rigs and state-of-the-art chairs. Eight of them were already filled, but there was an empty seat on the middle wall of screens, and I shivered, hoping and praying it was for me.

All of the players wore the fanciest VR headsets I'd ever seen, more like helmets than headsets. As I watched, I realised that what was on the screens was a projection of what the gamers were seeing on their headsets.

One was in a deep rainforest, another in space, while another was under the ocean. As I watched, a huge shark swam past and I heard the player swear as it frightened him, then he laughed softly.

Two members of staff wearing white clothes and dark glasses stood near each player. I guessed the screens were for them so they could see what the player was seeing without interrupting.

Weirdly, the room was almost silent. Now and then there would be a noise from one of the players, and there was sometimes whispering from the staff as they consulted together and made notes on their tablets. It took me a moment to understand what else was missing.

"I can't hear any tapping," I said to Conrad in a low voice. "They don't have controllers."

"They don't need them," he replied. "I'll let Margot explain – she's the expert."

I looked around the room again.

"What is this place?" I asked.

"One of the Foundation's research hubs. This is the Project C hub. You'll start here so you can get a feel for the project and learn how it works. You should be a natural at it. Dagmar says it's like a mashup of *Minecraft* and some of the better role-playing games, whatever that means." Conrad shrugged.

I knew *exactly* what that meant.

"Are you serious?" I said, my voice loud in the quiet. I was going to get to game? On this set-up? This was the best camp *ever*.

A couple of the staff looked over and spotted us. One of them hurried over – a woman with dark brown hair in a knot on top of her head and small glasses.

"Hi, I'm Margot. You must be Ivy," she said to me, tucking her tablet under her arm and holding out her hand. "I'm so happy to meet you."

"You too," I said as we shook hands. "This is incredible. The whole place. You'd never know it was here."

"Exactly the point," Margot said. "The old owners built it as a bomb shelter during the Second World War."

"It's why my aunt wanted to buy Chalmers Hall," Conrad explained. "Where better to conduct secret research than in a secret bunker? She designed everything. It's all her vision."

I couldn't imagine the amount of money or resources it must have taken. Dagmar had talked about "normal people like us", but she clearly had a lot more cash than my family.

"Are you ready to begin, Ivy?" Margot said to me, holding out an arm to guide me to the empty rig.

"I don't actually know what I'm doing," I admitted.

"It's all really easy, especially for someone like you. You don't need a crash course in how cyber worlds work," Margot laughed. "We're starting you in one of the Novo Reality spaces."

"What's that?" I asked, hovering by the chair.

"Well, you've heard of virtual reality and assisted reality and augmented reality?" Margot asked, and I nodded. "Novo Reality is the next step, and probably the ultimate one. Novo takes the user beyond a standard computer-generated universe and into their own personal reality that's created in digital form. Eventually, a user will be able to move seamlessly between the two, or even stay in Novo Reality if they prefer."

I shook my head, struggling to believe this. "How? What about life and jobs and food?"

"Well, Novo Reality is designed for a better future than the one we're currently heading towards," Margot replied. "One that includes a universal basic income and a comprehensive system for nutrient delivery, which we're currently successfully trialling."

It sounded like something from science fiction. I looked at Conrad, who shrugged as if to say, *I don't get it any more than you do*.

"How does it work?" I asked. I didn't understand how it could make my personal reality.

"Novo Reality works by using your actual brainwaves and thoughts to reconstruct the world as you imagine it. It also stimulates your receptors so you can feel and smell and taste what you've made, if you want to."

"Are you serious?" I said.

Margot nodded. "In Novo Reality, you have complete control over your environment – the only limit is your imagination. No adverts, no product placement, no influencers." Margot gave Conrad a look, and he held up his hands in mock-innocence. Then she turned back to me. "The headset basically reads your mind and projects an image of what you're thinking, which you see in the headset and we can see on the screens." Margot pointed to the ocean screen. "What's happening over there is happening inside the tester's mind. He's making it with his thoughts."

"That's impossible," I said, but my fingers were inching towards the headset, desperate to see if she was right. Of course you wouldn't need controllers if you could simply use your mind.

"Why don't you test it for yourself?" Margot said, handing the headset to me. "We'll get you comfortable in your seat ..."

Before she'd even finished speaking, I was sitting down and pulling the headset on.

Margot laughed. "I love the enthusiasm. But you need gloves. These will help you in the beginning. Our research shows us people find it hard to lie back and simply imagine. They need to use their hands a little to help make it feel real."

She handed me a pair of lightweight gloves covered in tiny black dots – sensors, I guessed.

When I'd put them on, Margot reached out and pulled the headset down over my face. The world went dark.

"Can you still hear me?" she asked, and I jumped. It had sounded as if her voice came from inside my head.

"Yes," I said.

"OK. I want you to picture an apple in your mind. Can you do that?"

I nodded, and an apple appeared before me.

It was perfect – deep red and shiny against the blackness.

"Very good, Ivy. Now take it," Margot's voice said.

I lifted my hand and jumped again as it appeared in my field of vision. It was my hand, my *actual* hand, right down to the freckles along the back and my short, stubby fingernails. I looked down and saw myself too, in the outfit I'd put on that morning: jeans and my hoodie. I held up my other hand and saw the scar on my finger from when I'd picked up a knife by the blade after my mom had dropped it when I'd been eight years old.

"Oh my god," I said. "They're my hands."

I heard Margot laughing.

"Take the apple," she reminded me, and I reached for it.

I felt the weight in my hand as if I was really holding the apple.

I didn't need Margot to tell me to take a bite.

The tart, sweet taste of fresh apple burst onto my tongue.

I chewed and swallowed, eating the whole thing. I held the core in my hand, and then imagined a rubbish bin, tossing the core into it.

"I can see you don't need my assistance at all," Margot said. "We'll leave you to it. Have fun."

But I'd stopped listening as I imagined myself an entire world.

*

It felt like only an hour had passed when someone shook my arm, and I pushed them away. I was in the middle of recreating the Cornish seaside my parents and I had visited last summer. I was just adjusting the blue of the sea when someone took the headset off me.

"Hey," I said, blinking as the real world flooded back in. "I wasn't finished."

Conrad was smiling at me, Margot next to him.

"It's time to go," Conrad said.

"I don't want lunch – I'm not hungry. Let me back in." I held out my hand for the headset.

"You can come back tomorrow. It's dinnertime now," Conrad said with a laugh.

I stared at him. "It can't be."

But as soon as he said it, I became aware my mouth was dry – really dry. My tongue was sticking to the roof of my mouth.

Margot handed me a large bottle of water.

"Drink it slowly," she said, and I obeyed, taking small sips.

"You've been in Novo Reality for almost nine hours," Conrad said when the water was gone.

My jaw dropped. How was that possible? How hadn't I noticed I was thirsty, or hungry, or hadn't needed the bathroom? I hadn't needed anything while I was in there. It had been just me and Novo Reality.

And the weirdest thing was that I wanted to go straight back in. The idea of having to be out in the real world was horrible.

"What do you think?" Margot asked.

"I love it," I said. "Can I come back after dinner? Just to finish something? I'll be quick."

Conrad and Margot looked at each other. "Not tonight," Margot said. "But Dagmar does sometimes make exceptions for really promising participants. You might be able to stay later another time."

I bit my tongue to stop myself from saying it wasn't fair, that I just needed a bit longer. Instead, I forced myself to nod. I would convince Dagmar I was the most promising participant they'd ever had. Anything to get back to Novo Reality.

My legs were shaky when I stood up. Conrad had to steady me, which would normally have made me blush, but I was still consumed by the world I'd built, thinking of all the things I had left to do.

"Did you see it on the screen?" I asked Conrad as we climbed the stairs and left the folly. "It was the most incredible thing. I made so much: the theme park we went to on a school trip in my last year at primary school, and the Empire State Building – I made the *freaking Empire State Building!*"

"Shh," Conrad hushed me, but he was smiling. "Remember it's supposed to be a secret."

"Sorry, sorry," I said, but a second later I was talking again, loud and fast, excitement buzzing in me. "And Central Park – we went to New York for my parents' twentieth wedding anniversary, and it was amazing to be able to see it all again, to walk around and feel like I was really there. I'm going to try making Hyrule tomorrow. That's the kingdom where the *Zelda* series is set. How weird will that be – to be able to walk inside it as if I'm Link?"

I stopped walking as a wild thought occurred to me.

"Do you think I can *fly* in there?" I asked.

"I think you can do anything," Conrad said. "Now hush – we need to get inside without being seen. Dagmar is excited to hear about your first day."

We rounded the corner and Chalmers Hall came into view. After checking the coast was clear, we crept up the driveway and inside, heading straight to Dagmar's office.

"What do think of our little project?" Dagmar asked me.

"I think it's everything," I said, and Dagmar smiled.

"We agree," she said. "It's going to change the way people use online space. We're planning the next stage of the project now."

"What's that?" I asked.

"Imagine if you could share your world with another user. Invite them in and visit theirs. Imagine if you could collaborate together, join your worlds and work with each other to build something entirely new. Forget the Metaverse, forget those silly flights-to-Mars simulators," Dagmar said. "Forget all of that nonsense. We're going to beat them all, and what's more, we're not going to charge anyone a penny for it. Not one cent."

I stared at Dagmar. "How is that possible?"

Dagmar smiled. "We won't need to. When the other developers see what we have here, they'll drop their vanity projects and beg us to let them get involved with the Foundation. And then everyone will follow. Just think what we can do when we get the whole world online! We can make something really beautiful. There is no climate disaster or war or famine in Novo Reality, unless people imagine it, but why would they when they can make and control their own paradise? Unlike in the real world, the only limit in there is your imagination. Novo Reality means true equality. And who doesn't want to be part of that?"

I didn't realise how hard I was nodding until my neck started to hurt.

CHAPTER 11

Conrad and I had missed dinner, so Dagmar had the staff send some food up to our rooms.

I wasn't hungry, despite the fact I hadn't eaten real food all day. I'd been eating in Novo Reality, recreating the pastrami sandwich I'd had from the famous sandwich shop in New York, right down to the mustard that had dripped on my T-shirt. I knew it wasn't real, but it had left me feeling satisfied in a way the Foundation's spaghetti carbonara couldn't.

I couldn't stop thinking about Novo Reality. Every bit of me wanted to be back inside it, exploring and creating. I put the tray of pasta I'd been sent on the floor and lay down on the bed, closing my eyes and pretending I was back underneath the folly, hooked up to the screens. I imagined all the things I could make and do – I could recreate and star in my favourite games, add new levels and bosses, even make entirely new games and test them out. Dagmar was right: imagination was the limit. Novo Reality really would change the whole world.

Especially if it was free. I couldn't imagine any other company in the world giving away something as huge and exciting as Novo Reality and not charging anything for it. It really would make everyone equal. It wouldn't matter if you were a billionaire in the real world – in Novo Reality you'd only be as good as what you could dream up. And nothing I'd seen made me think billionaires dreamed of anything but more money, which was useless in Novo Reality.

I fell asleep in my clothes, my mind inside its own inferior version of Novo Reality. I couldn't wait to get back there.

*

The next morning, I was awake and ready to go by six, pacing the hallway outside Dagmar's office as I waited for Conrad to appear.

"You're up early," said Dagmar, coming out of the dining room, a cup of coffee in her hand.

"Just really excited to get started," I said. "Do you know if Conrad is awake?"

"I don't, but I can walk you over to the folly once you've had breakfast if he's still not about."

"I'm not hungry," I said.

Dagmar gave me a stern look. "Ivy, Novo Reality is exciting, and I'm delighted you're so enthusiastic, but you still have to nourish your human body, at least until we've perfected the sustenance patches."

"What are those?" I asked. "Is that the nutrient system Margot was talking about? Do you need more volunteers?"

Dagmar burst out laughing. "We will definitely keep you in mind, Ivy."

*

After I'd munched on a croissant with Nutella and gulped down some coffee, Dagmar escorted me down to the folly, where she handed me over to Margot.

I was surprised to see the other testers were already there, inside Novo Reality.

"Who are they?" I asked Margot as she helped me put my gloves on.

"Other volunteers. They're not part of the programme you were here for, so you don't need to worry about them."

I looked more closely at them and realised they were all wearing the same clothes they'd had on the day before.

"They didn't go home yesterday, did they?" I asked. "Were they inside Novo Reality all night?"

"They're at a much more advanced stage of engagement with Novo Reality than you are," Margot said, holding the headset out to me. "They've been working with it for some time. Now, let's see what you can do today."

I pulled the headset on and entered Novo Reality.

*

I assumed it was dinnertime when Margot pulled me out, and I was annoyed to find it was only lunchtime.

"I don't need lunch; I'm still full from breakfast," I said, reaching for the headset to go back into Novo Reality.

"Ms Nilsson made it clear that you have to take proper breaks to use the bathroom and to eat and rehydrate," Margot explained.

"I said I'm fine," I replied, and held out my hands for my headset.

"I'll have to let Ms Nilsson know about this," Margot said.

"Tell her," I replied, the headset already covering my eyes as I stepped back inside my own personal world. A moment later, I spread my arms and leaped into the sky.

*

"Ivy, we need to talk," Dagmar said later, when she came to fetch me before dinner. "You put Margot in a very difficult position earlier. She's there not just to monitor the work but to keep you safe."

I realised I hadn't seen Conrad all day and that I hadn't even thought of him.

"I know. I'm sorry. But I don't need to take a lunch break," I said, trying to look as if I was sorry. "I'm happy in there."

"And you feel all right?" Dagmar asked as we climbed the stairs out of the bunker.

I staggered, almost tripping up the stairs, as if the question had put a curse on me.

"I'm fine," I lied.

So what if I had a mild headache from not drinking any water? So what if my stomach felt hollow? Novo Reality and spending as much time in it as possible was the only thing I cared about. I'd have to go home in three weeks, and then who knew when I'd next be able to get in?

"Ivy, I can see that you're not," Dagmar said.

"How do the others do it?" I asked. "How do they stay in there? They do, don't they? They're wearing the exact same clothes as yesterday."

Dagmar sighed. "I told you – the sustenance patches. That batch of volunteers are the testers for them."

"Let me test them too," I begged. "They're all fine, aren't they? Dagmar – Ms Nilsson – please."

Dagmar paused by the shore of the lake. In the early evening sun, it was beautiful, but all I could think was that if I recreated it inside Novo Reality, I could edit out the wisps of dark cloud that were ruining the orange and pink sky. I could add a pair of swans, or maybe even flamingos. In Novo Reality, I could make it better. I could make it perfect.

"I don't know, Ivy." Dagmar paused. "Let me think about it. In the meantime, you have to go and eat a proper dinner. I'll ask the staff to tell me what you ate. Come to my office at nine. I'll let you know what I've decided."

"Thank you. Thank you," I said again.

*

"Ivy, oh my god, where have you been?" Ruby called out.

Ruby and Freya came racing over to me as soon as they saw me enter the dining room. They were the only two people in there, besides the staff – it looked like everyone else had already eaten and left.

"Just doing outdoor stuff. It's really tiring," I said as I snagged a slice of pizza and some chips.

I saw them giving each other another knowing look, but I didn't care. When I sat down, they sat with me.

The pizza tasted flat to me after the food I'd imagined eating in Novo Reality, as if this was the fake world and in there was real. If it wasn't for Dagmar's order, I would have stopped eating, but I could feel the staff in white watching me. I knew I had to finish the whole plate to give me a chance of getting onto the sustenance-patch test.

"How was cooking?" I asked them.

"We thought you'd signed up for it too," Freya said.

"I crossed my name out. I thought the outside stuff might be a bit much."

"What did you do while we were working our butts off over a hot stove?" Ruby asked.

"Nothing much," I said. "Just noodled around. Went for a walk."

"Were you with Conrad?" Freya said, not quite meeting my eye.

I remembered what Conrad had told me about her. The stalking and the crimes and the way she'd almost ruined Hye-jin's life.

"Are you all right?" Ruby asked. "Are you in pain? You've gone really pale."

"I'm fine," I managed to reply, stuffing a handful of chips into my mouth. "Just hungry."

I didn't speak for the rest of the meal, pretending to focus on my food while Ruby chatted and Freya nodded at her. Every now and then, Freya shot a glance at me, and I felt myself flushing before I looked away. I emptied the plate in no time, desperate to get away from her.

"I'm going to get brownies," Ruby said. "Do you want a normal one or a weird one? There are some with currants in, and while I respect that as an artistic choice, I wouldn't eat them."

"A normal brownie would be great," I said.

"Good choice." Ruby dashed off, leaving me with Freya.

"He told you about me, didn't he?" she said in a soft voice. "That's why you've been avoiding us."

"I don't know what you're talking about," I said. "I'm not avoiding you. You both left me at dinner the other night and didn't come back. We just have different schedules. It's not a big deal."

"Ivy, I think you should be careful," Freya warned. "I know you don't trust me right now, but I think—"

"Gotta go. Talk later."

Before she could say anything else, I chased after Ruby, snatching up two brownies.

"See you," I said to an astonished Ruby.

Then I fled the dining room, heading to my bedroom to wait until nine, when I'd find out Dagmar's decision.

CHAPTER 12

"I've decided that you can join the sustenance-patch trial," Dagmar said the moment I opened the door to her office. "Margot said the work you've been doing is really advanced. She reported that you mastered flight shortly before lunchtime today. Do you know, it took the others over a month before they thought to imagine flying, let alone mastered it? It seems you're made for Novo Reality, Ivy."

If the desk hadn't been between us, I might have hugged Dagmar, but instead I settled for grinning and clasping my hands together.

"Thank you," I said, unable to stop smiling. "You won't regret it. Just wait until you see what else I can do."

"I believe it." Dagmar laughed. "Like I said the other night, I'm very good at spotting potential."

"What do I do now? What happens next?" I asked.

"Tomorrow, first thing, I'll take you over to the folly … Unless you want to go now?" Dagmar said.

I'd tried not to pull a face, to keep my expression normal, but I didn't want to wait until tomorrow. I wanted to get back in there now, especially after what had happened with Freya.

"Can I?"

Dagmar sighed, then shrugged. "All right. If that's what you really want."

"It is," I replied.

*

An hour later, I was sitting back in my chair in the folly, staring at the pair of needles Margot was holding up.

"Are you all right?" Dagmar asked.

"I didn't realise the sustenance was going to be an IV," I said. "I thought it was a patch."

"We can't deliver the nutrients you need using a patch. Not yet," Dagmar clarified. "But it's not uncomfortable. A slight pinch to insert them, and then you won't feel a thing."

"How does it work?" I asked.

"The one in your left arm provides all your nutrients and fluids; the other in your right is connected to a machine that will clean your blood of any excess nutrients so you don't have to use the bathroom. It's our own invention. We based the technology on plasma donation. When you donate plasma, the machine takes out whole blood, extracts the plasma and then returns the blood to you. Our machine works in a similar way. It's very clever."

I swallowed.

Suddenly, I was nervous. I hadn't really thought about things like needing the bathroom. Still, I supposed a system to clean my blood was better than having to wear a nappy or being brought out of Novo Reality every time I needed to go.

"Is it safe?" I asked.

"Look around you," Dagmar said, and I did.

I hadn't noticed before that all the other players had tubes going into their arms. It didn't seem to be hurting them or stopping them from working.

"How long do they stay in?" I said.

"The staff will change the fluid and nutrient packs three times a day, but you shouldn't notice. They won't touch the cannulas – the tubes in your arm. What's the longest someone has stayed in Novo Reality for, Margot?" Dagmar asked her.

"Six days," Margot replied. "Most testers take a break every forty-eight hours to stretch their real-world legs, but Ryan stayed in for six days while he was reconstructing the pyramids of Giza and the Sphinx." Margot pointed at a boy with blue hair on the opposite side of the room. His fingers were moving rapidly in the air. "He wanted to get it just right. And he did."

"But it's not a competition," Dagmar said firmly. "If you want to come out after an hour, that's OK."

I nodded slowly. "All right. Let's do this."

I sat in the chair and breathed deeply as Margot inserted a cannula into my left arm, and then one into the other. It didn't hurt, but it did feel weird, and even stranger when Margot hooked the cannulas up to the machines. I felt a cold rush in my left arm as the fluids and nutrients were delivered, and a faint tug in my right as the cleaning process started, but I soon got used to it.

"All set?" Dagmar asked, handing me my headset.

"All set," I replied, and then pulled it on.

A moment later, I was in the sky in Novo Reality, soaring and looping. I imagined how it must look to Dagmar, watching me on the screens. Then I forgot about Dagmar, the tubes in my arm and the real world. I had work to do.

*

I built castles and temples, oceans and forests and deserts and mountains and rivers. I imagined horses and wolves and golden eagles. I even flew with the eagles, soaring with them over huge meadows I built in my mind. I recreated a totally new *Legend of Zelda* game, mapping out all of Hyrule and the surrounding areas and then adding in new things – things that had never appeared in the real games. I called it *Legend of Zelda: The Wind Grail*. The point of the game was to rescue Zelda but also to reunite the four pieces of the Wind Grail to defeat Ganon, the bad guy, and save Hyrule. I played it through the way I wished I could play games at home – without stopping. This was everything I'd ever dreamed of.

Every so often, Margot would interrupt me, her voice booming in my head from the outside world, asking me if I needed a break – if I wanted to stop. I felt her moving my legs, bending them at the knee and stretching them, and I tried to kick her away as I focused on my work.

Another time I thought I heard Dagmar, her voice picked up by Margot's microphone. Dagmar was telling Margot to leave me alone – that if I chose to stay in Novo Reality that was my business, and this was the point of the test.

I tuned them both out when Margot started to argue. I didn't have time to listen to their silly real-world problems. I had my own worlds to manage here.

*

The first I knew that something was wrong was when I felt a sharp, terrible pain in my right arm, and then again in my left. I looked down at my arms in Novo Reality and saw they were bleeding. A second later, they vanished as someone pulled the headset from my face, yanking me back into reality. Margot was standing in front of me, just a dark outline in front of the screens.

"Come on," she hissed. "We have to go. Now, before the others come back."

"What?" I said, but no sound came from my mouth, my voice nothing more than a scratch. I tried again, but only a rasp of noise came out.

Margot pulled me from my chair, and my legs collapsed under me. She caught me before I hit the floor and tried to make me stand, but I couldn't put any weight on my feet. It felt as if all the bones in my lower body had turned to liquid and were sloshing around inside my skin.

In the end, Margot hooked her arm around me and dragged me to the door. I tried to fight her, tried to scream for help, but none of me was working the way it was supposed to – my legs and arms were floppy and useless, my voice a scratchy whisper.

I looked around and saw that everyone else was still in Novo Reality, and I wanted to be there too. There were no other staff there, no people in white. Nothing made sense in the real world, and I hated it.

Somehow, Margot got me up the stairs and out into the folly. It was night-time, and the moon was full. Something about it started an alarm ringing in my head – it meant something important. But it was hard to focus when I was being pulled out into the cold air and I couldn't do anything to stop it.

"I've got her," Margot said. "She can't walk, so we're going to have to carry her to my car. Wait here with her. I'll try to bring it closer."

"Jesus Christ," a familiar voice said. "What have they done to her?"

"Ruby?" I mouthed.

Ruby's face appeared before mine. "You look terrible, Ivy. Are you OK?"

"What's happening?" I asked, my voice barely a whisper. My throat was starting to hurt.

"She needs water," someone else said. It was Freya, and a moment later she was holding a bottle to my lips. "Careful," she said, tipping it up so I could only take sips.

The water was so good. I tried to take it from her, but my arms were weak, and she pushed me away easily.

"What's happening?" I said again when Freya took the water away. My voice was a little better – still faint and scratchy, but it was there at least. "What's wrong with me?"

"What's wrong with you is that you've been sitting in a seat all this time, working away as some test puppet for a maniac," Ruby said. "A megalomaniac. You haven't used your legs for so long that all your strength is gone."

"But it's only been a few days," I said.

Freya and Ruby looked at each other.

"Ivy, you've been missing for a month."

CHAPTER 13

I stared at Ruby and Freya.

"What are you talking about?" I asked. "I'm not missing. I'm right here. I've always been here."

"We didn't know that," Freya said. "Dagmar told everyone you'd run away. Your mums have been at Chalmers Hall almost every day, and the police are involved. There was a huge search for you, Ivy. People in the grounds with dogs and sticks, looking for you."

"We have to go back and tell everyone I'm OK," I said. "Why did Margot leave us here? Wait, why didn't she tell the police where I was? She knew."

Freya and Ruby looked at each other.

"I hate it when you do that," I said. "It makes me feel like an outsider."

"Sorry," Ruby and Freya chorused. "You'd better explain," Freya said to Ruby.

Ruby took a deep breath. "So, we didn't believe you'd run away. It didn't make sense because it was clear something was happening between you and Conrad—"

"And when the police found out about that, they started questioning him," Freya cut across Ruby.

"Do you want to tell the story instead?" Ruby asked Freya, and Freya rolled her eyes. "All right. *As I was saying* ... Everyone had seen Conrad with you, and we all had to talk to the police, so they knew. Conrad told them you'd misunderstood and he was trying to be nice, but you'd tried to kiss him—"

"What?" I shrieked, hurting my throat.

"And he'd rejected you, so that's why you ran away," Ruby said. "He had an alibi, so they weren't blaming him exactly. But they were suspicious."

"And so were we," Freya added, unable to stop herself joining in. "You were acting so weird that last day, and Conrad and Dagmar were being strange too. So we broke into Dagmar's office, and boom!"

"Boom?" I repeated weakly. "What do you mean by 'boom'? And can I have some more water?"

Freya handed me the bottle, and I sipped slowly as Ruby continued.

"I know he told you about Freya, but did Conrad tell you why I came here?" Ruby asked, and I shook my head. "It's because I downloaded an app that turned out to be fake, and I got stalked by the maker and almost murdered in my own home. *Guess who* gave him the funding for the app?"

I shook my head, but I knew in my stomach what she was about to say.

"The Ash Tree Foundation," Freya said. "The same people who developed the AdelAIDE AI assistant that data-scraped my life and advised me to commit crimes to get popular. And there's more. They've funded dozens of projects – in fact, all the people who were at the camp were there because of something the Ash Tree Foundation paid for that went really wrong."

"How do you know this?" I asked.

Ruby snorted. "For a tech maniac, Dagmar is useless with her security. She'd closed her laptop, but when we opened it, the lockscreen hadn't activated, so we could see everything. Access all her files. We ran a search for you and found out you were in the folly testing Novo Reality."

"The stuff she'd written about you was horrible," Freya said with a shudder. "The plans they had for you. The things they were going to do."

I held up a trembling hand. "I don't want to know. Not now."

"Fair enough."

"We had no idea what the folly was," Ruby picked up the story again, "but when we got home, I went to Freya's, and we looked it up online. We found out there was a folly on the grounds of Chalmers Hall, and so we came back."

"I live nearby," Freya explained.

"We found the folly," Ruby continued, "but we couldn't see how you could be here. Still, it was the only lead we had, so we kept coming back, trying to solve it while the police did nothing useful." Ruby rolled her eyes.

"And then we saw that woman, Margot, coming here," Freya said. "We watched her open the tomb and go in. We couldn't find how she did it, so we waited for her to come out and we ambushed her. We told her we'd recorded her going in and sent the video to my sister, and if she didn't tell us what was down there or tried to hurt us, my sister would go straight to the police," Freya said.

"Margot crumbled like a week-old cookie," Ruby added with satisfaction. "She confessed you were down there and that she was worried about you, but her boss had threatened her family if she told the police anything. So then we said that if she didn't help us get you out, we'd release the recording we'd made of her confession online," Ruby said. "There wasn't really a recording of it, but she didn't know that. After that, Margot told us that there was a full staff meeting so everyone could get their stories straight, but someone had to stay with the testers, so she volunteered. And here we are. Operation Save Ivy is a huge success. Or it will be once we get you out of here and to the police."

"Margot's been gone a long time," Freya said, looking around.

"We have to help the others," I said. "There's eight other people down there, and they've been there longer than me. Wait!" I added. "This is only one of the projects. Project C, Conrad told me. Which means there must be Projects A and B somewhere else."

"Ivy, we can't worry about that now," Ruby said. "And we only have room in the getaway car for you. I promise we'll tell the police where they are and about the other projects. They'll be OK." Ruby rubbed my arm.

"I think Margot is on her way back," Freya said, standing up. "I can hear someone coming."

"About time," Ruby said, rising too.

I tried to stand, but my legs were like lumps of meat beneath me. I could move them, but they wouldn't take my weight.

Freya was frowning. "That sounds like more than one person, doesn't it?"

"No," Ruby said, but she was frowning too. "Oh no. We have to hide."

But it was too late. A second later, I saw Dagmar's white-blonde hair and white clothes glowing in the light of the moon as a dozen Foundation staff members rushed towards us.

"Run!" I told Ruby and Freya.

"Not without you," Freya said.

"We're in this together, Ivy," Ruby said. "If they take you back, they have to take us too."

CHAPTER 14

Ruby and Freya didn't try to fight or run, but the Foundation staff still gagged them and tied them up. They forced them to walk while a man carried me in his arms like a baby. They didn't tie my wrists – clearly they didn't think I'd be able to do any damage or escape in this state. When I tried to scream, only air came out. Dagmar didn't say a word – she didn't even look at me, simply giving instructions to her staff in a low, steady voice as we were taken back to Chalmers Hall.

"Find Margot," Dagmar commanded. "And send someone to her home. I want Margot's family brought here so she understands the stakes. And take these three into the ballroom. I'll be there shortly."

My blood ran cold at the stony look on Dagmar's face.

The staff took us to the ballroom and sat us apart: Freya by the window, Ruby in the middle and me on the far side. Two of the staff stayed, guarding the door.

I looked over at Ruby and Freya.

"Are you OK?" I asked, my voice barely a whisper.

"No talking," one of the staff snapped, "or we'll gag you too."

Ruby was clearly furious, her black curls shivering with outrage. If looks could kill, the people watching us would surely be dead. Freya met my eye and gave a swift nod, then she looked down at the floor as if she was trying to make herself small.

None of this felt real. Was that because Novo Reality was still hijacking my brain? If this was Novo Reality, I could simply imagine away the gag. I could imagine my friends safe and my parents ...

At the thought of my mom and mum, I jolted back into reality. They must be so worried and feel so guilty. What if I never saw them again?

The door opened and Dagmar strolled inside. Conrad was with her.

"You have to know I can't let you leave here," Dagmar said.

Behind her gag, Ruby snarled something at Dagmar.

"The work is too important. You understand, don't you, Ivy?" Dagmar looked at me. "You've seen what we're doing here. I told you what I'm hoping to do. What it will mean."

This time Freya said something, and Dagmar sighed.

"Take the gags off," Dagmar said. "I suppose the least I can do is hear their insults."

Two of the staff stepped forward and removed Ruby and Freya's gags.

"You won't get away with this," Ruby hissed.

"I can assure you we very much will *get away with it*, as you say, you silly girl. You see, we're backed by some of the most important people in the world, people who are deeply invested in us and what we're doing here. They don't mind if we make mistakes. They just ask us to clean them up."

Ruby sucked in a sharp breath and fell silent.

"And what did you say?" Dagmar turned to Freya.

"I said 'you ruined my life'," Freya replied in a calm, even voice. "But at least now I know how it all got hushed up – your investors and those important people made it all go away."

"Yes," Dagmar said simply. "That's how it works."

"You're not human," Freya said. "You can't be. The things you've paid for: AdelAIDE, the app that almost got Ruby killed, everything else. You're disgusting, experimenting on people without their consent."

"*You* ruined your life," Dagmar said. "Wasting your time wanting to be popular like my nephew. Selling your soul for a crumb of attention. You didn't have to do a single thing the AI suggested – you chose to, Freya. But you did get some great results for us, so I should thank you. We've been able to develop a much better AI assistant model because of you."

"How can you do this?" Freya accused Conrad. He hadn't looked at any of us since he'd come into the room, staring at the window instead as if he was bored. "This is evil."

Conrad ignored her.

Finally, I spoke. "You were using me."

Everyone in the room looked at me, even Conrad.

"Yes, Ivy. If you want to put it like that, I suppose I was using you," Dagmar said. "The only reason we let you come was so I could use you. You see, the work we're doing here is special."

"You mean it's unethical," Freya spat. "Margot told us you have people down there plugged into drips that feed them. They never go outside, never even log off."

"They're all volunteers, like Ivy," Dagmar said.

"They're all homeless," Freya snapped back. "Homeless youths, or they've come out of young offender institutions and don't have any other options. You're taking advantage of them."

"Is that true?" I asked Dagmar.

"Is that what this is?" Dagmar sneered at Freya, ignoring me. "Are you jealous we didn't choose you?"

"You wish," Freya spat.

"Is that true?" I asked again, my voice louder.

"Ivy, we're giving them a second chance," Dagmar said. "Society isn't kind to the unhoused, or to ex-offenders." Dagmar shot a glance at Freya. "What we're offering is a chance to really contribute to something that will benefit all humankind. To be useful."

"So why me?" I asked.

"Because you already have the right skills. Unfortunately, the volunteers we recruit haven't had the access to the games that you have, so they must be taught how they work and what the capabilities are. I told you: you mastered in less than a day what took some of them weeks to understand. With people like you helping us, we can reach our goal so much faster. We don't want to lose you, Ivy."

I was about to reply when a phone rang. Dagmar pulled a sleek, slim device from the pocket of her trousers.

"I hope this is good news," she said, then paused. "Excellent! Bring her in."

Dagmar ended the call.

"They've found Margot. They're fetching her now," Dagmar said to Conrad, who nodded. "Let's finish this."

Dagmar nodded at the staff, and they came over, pulling Ruby and Freya to their feet.

"What are you doing?" I said as Ruby and Freya tried to fight against the staff. "Leave them alone."

"You must see that I can't do that, Ivy," Dagmar said, turning to leave the room.

"I'll stay!" I shouted as loud as I could with my broken voice. "I'll stay here for ever if you let them go. I'll do whatever you want."

Dagmar paused.

"And will you two keep our secret here?" she asked Freya and Ruby.

"Go to hell," they said at the same time, and then grinned, even in the face of the danger they were in.

"There's your answer," Dagmar said. She left, followed by the staff who took Freya and Ruby with them.

"Do something!" I said to Conrad. "You can't let this happen. You know what she meant by 'clean up her mistakes', don't you? What she's going to do to them?"

"You don't understand," Conrad said, coming to sit a few seats away from me. "I told you my dad left when I was a baby. My mum and I don't have anything. Dagmar helps us."

"You have your platform!" I told him. "All the sponsorships and money!"

"It's not as much as you think," Conrad said bitterly. "Before Dagmar came along, we'd almost lost the house. We had nothing."

"She's going to kill them!" I said.

Conrad shifted in his seat, adjusting something in his pocket.

His phone.

He'd told me he had a phone.

If I could get it from him, I could call the police. I could save us.

"You know what really hurts," I began, not looking at him. "I thought you actually liked me."

"I do," Conrad said.

"Ha," I said. "Sure you do. Just like you're really against technology. I actually believed I'd found something amazing here. You. Novo Reality."

"You can still have it," Conrad said, moving a seat closer. "Dagmar thinks you're brilliant. She says the work you've done in just a month has pushed us years closer to finishing this stage. And I ... I really do like you."

"Yeah, right. You told me I'd got in because I was special. Put me in the blue room so I was separated from the others. You hid the orienteering sign-up sheet so no one else could join, didn't you?"

Conrad nodded.

"All of it, every bit, designed to flatter me into thinking I was special," I said.

"You are special."

"I feel like such a fool," I said as if Conrad hadn't spoken. "I can't believe I fell for another scam where I thought someone liked me."

"It's not a scam. Ivy ..." He shifted to the seat next to mine and took my hands. "I promise I like you," he said. "I faked a lot of things, but not that."

He leaned in to kiss me.

"What's that?" I asked, looking behind him.

"What?" Conrad pulled back and looked at the window.

"I thought I saw someone looking in."

Conrad turned to me, his face full of alarm. "You can't have," he said.

"There!" I pointed.

This time Conrad rose and went to the window.

"They were right there," I said.

He pressed his face against the glass, peering out. "Are you—"

But Conrad didn't get to finish his sentence because I picked up one of the ugly vases from the cabinet next to me and pitched it at his head.

My arms were weak and my aim terrible, but I managed to clip the side of his head, sending him staggering. It wasn't enough.

Conrad O'Connell turned to me. "You bitch," he said. "You tried to trick me."

He ran at me, his face full of rage. At the last minute, I twisted away, knocking my chair over with me still in it, my legs still mostly useless.

Conrad tripped over it, flying head-first into the cabinet, where he crumpled and lay still.

I dragged myself to him. His nose was bleeding, but when I checked his pulse, it was strong. I didn't have long.

I reached into Conrad's pocket and pulled out his phone, dialling 999.

"Hello, emergency service operator," came the voice on the line. "Which service do you require? Fire, police or ambulance?"

"Police," I said into the phone as Conrad moaned softly, already coming around. "I need the police."

"I'll just connect you now."

"Hello, Police, what's your name and where are you calling from?"

"I'm Ivy Finch. I'm the missing girl: Ivy Finch. I'm at Chalmers Hall. They kidnapped me and they have my friends. They're going to kill them. You have to come now!"

Conrad moaned again.

"OK, Ivy, try to keep calm and stay on the line," the police operator said.

"Just hurry," I replied. "I—"

The door to the ballroom flew open and I screamed, dropping the phone.

Ruby and Freya came running towards me, wrapping me in a group hug.

"Are you OK?" we all said at the same time.

"How did you get away?" I asked, unable to believe they were all right.

Ruby puffed out her chest.

"Well, I might be *a silly girl*, but I'm also smart enough to enrol in self-defence lessons after my stalker tried to kill me at home," she said. "I couldn't take on so many of them by the lake, but two was fairly easy. Dagmar and one of those other cult freaks just had their asses thoroughly kicked." She looked at Conrad, still on the floor, and grinned. "I see you know exactly what I'm talking about."

"You two," Freya said, pulling us both into another hug.

We heard the sound of sirens racing towards Chalmers Hall.

CHAPTER 15

Ruby stood on my bed, wearing my dressing gown with a towel wrapped around her head like a headscarf. Three months had passed since that terrible night at Chalmers Hall when I thought Ruby and Freya were going to be killed and I'd probably be hooked back up to Novo Reality for ever.

"What's the line?" she said.

"Erm …" I looked down at my copy of the script. "*When I was at home with Papa …*"

But instead of continuing the monologue, Ruby threw herself onto my bed with a grunt.

"This isn't getting my juices flowing," she said. "Do you have any snacks? Maybe I'll be better with chocolate."

"I'll go and see, but be warned, my mom is on some anti-ultra-processed food thing, so we probably only have fruit."

I left Ruby muttering lines to herself and headed downstairs. I was at school with Ruby now. She'd come over to my house so we could practise our monologues for GCSE Drama. Freya would be here soon too, and the three of us would order pizza if my mom wasn't home, or make pesto pasta and salad if she was. After everything that had happened, it was hardly surprising that we'd become really good friends. As Ruby had put it: "nothing is quite as bonding as almost being murdered by evil tech barons hell-bent on ruling the world".

Somehow, Dagmar and Conrad had got away. We didn't understand how. We'd left Conrad on the ballroom floor, barely conscious, as the first officers arrived on the scene. But he'd still disappeared from right under their noses. There'd been no sign of him since, and his social media channels had all disappeared, like he'd never existed.

To make things worse, the investigators hadn't found evidence of any other projects, but that might have been because Dagmar's laptop had disappeared when she did. The police tried to convince me that there weren't any other sites, that Conrad had been lying to make it sound more impressive. But I'd been inside the Foundation. Dagmar's work was everything to her. I knew there were other sites – that somewhere out there the Foundation was still running.

Freya thought that some of the police were probably being paid off by the Foundation and they'd let Conrad escape, maybe even helped him. Dagmar too. They couldn't have got away on their own.

All of the other staff, including Margot, had been arrested, but she was the only one who had agreed to testify against the Foundation. The rest refused to say a word. The hub underneath the folly was dismantled and the other testers all freed. But who knows what they went back to, if Dagmar had been telling the truth about them.

I didn't really play games any more, but sometimes – most nights, to be truthful – I still dreamed I was in Novo Reality, where I could do and make and be anything. I'd never admit it to anyone, but I missed it.

"Chocolate?" I heard Ruby call from upstairs.

There was none in the usual cupboard, but when I checked the box of Bran Flakes on top of the fridge, I found a bar hidden inside and smiled. Mom might be against ultra-processed food, but my mum wouldn't let anything stand between her and her cravings.

"Ivy!" Ruby screamed.

"I'm coming," I said. "Calm down."

I heard footsteps thundering down the stairs and Ruby appeared, her face pale.

"Forget the chocolate," she said, holding her phone out to me. "Look."

I stared at the screen, and the chocolate slipped from my hand.

"*Conrad O'Connell spotted near Chalmers Hall*" the headline read.

"He's back," Ruby said.

Who is hiding behind Ruby's
new **ECHOSTAR** app?

MELINDA SALISBURY

ECHOSTAR
IS ALWAYS
LISTENING

"Smart, witty and utterly terrifying" SIMON JAMES GREEN

978-1-80090-270-1

What happens when new **AI**
TECHNOLOGY proves too powerful?

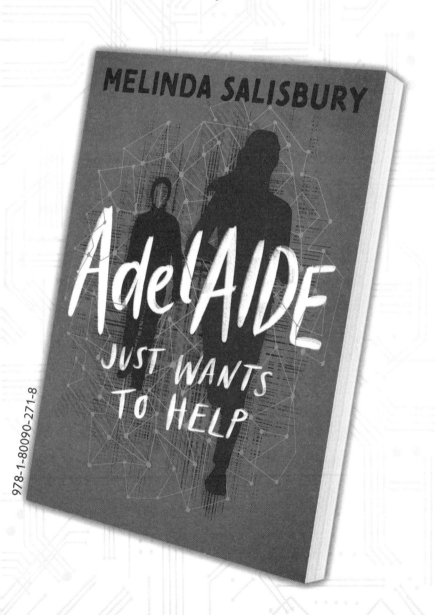

978-1-80090-271-8

MELINDA SALISBURY

AdelAIDE
JUST WANTS
TO HELP

Our books are tested
for children and young people by
children and young people.

Thanks to everyone who consulted on
a manuscript for their time and effort in
helping us to make our books better
for our readers.